POWER CODERS

OUR MINECRAFT UNICORN

AMANDA VINK

ILLUSTRATED BY JOEL GENNARI

PowerKiDS press

Published in 2019 by The Rosen Publishing Group, Inc.
29 East 21st Street, New York, NY 10010

First Edition

Illustrator: Joel Gennari
Minecraft Illustrator: Matías Lapegüe
Interior Layout: Tanya Dellaccio
Editorial Director: Greg Roza

Cataloging-in-Publishing Data
Names: Vink, Amanda.
Title: Our Minecraft unicorn / Amanda Vink.
Description: New York : PowerKids Press, 2019. | Series: Power coders | Includes glossary and index.
Identifiers: ISBN 9781725301849 (pbk.) | ISBN 9781725301863 (library bound) | ISBN 9781725301856 (6pack)
Subjects: LCSH: Computer programmers–Juvenile fiction. |Minecraft (Game)–Juvenile fiction. | Unicorns–Juvenile fiction.
Classification: LCC PZ7.V565 Ou 2019 | DDC [E]–dc23

Manufactured in the United States of America

CPSIA Compliance Information: Batch CWPK19. For Further Information contact Rosen Publishing, New York, New York at 1-800-237-9932

CONTENTS

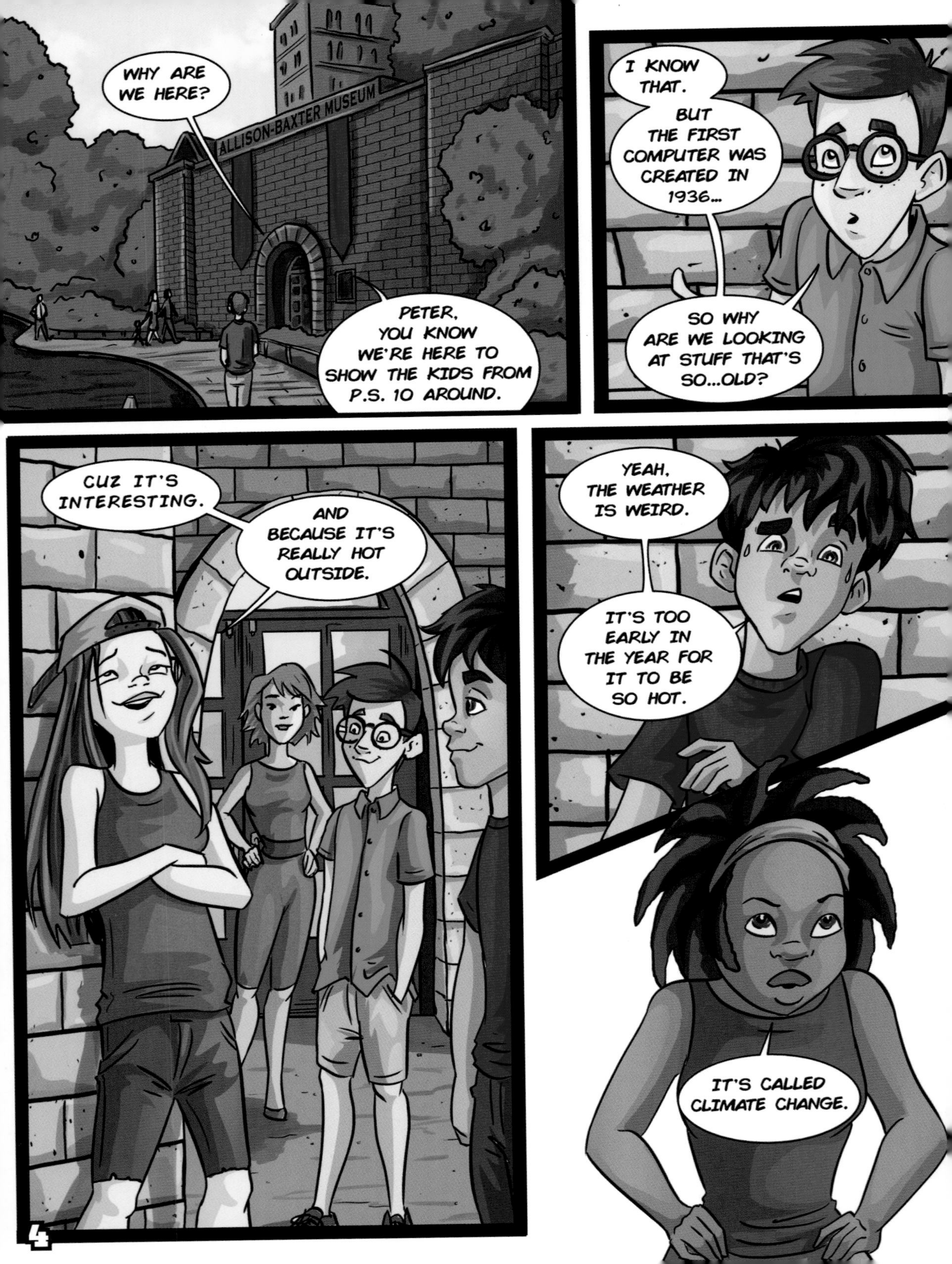
ALLISON-BAXTER MUSEUM
WHY ARE WE HERE?
PETER, YOU KNOW WE'RE HERE TO SHOW THE KIDS FROM P.S. 10 AROUND.
I KNOW THAT.
BUT THE FIRST COMPUTER WAS CREATED IN 1936...
SO WHY ARE WE LOOKING AT STUFF THAT'S SO...OLD?
CUZ IT'S INTERESTING.
AND BECAUSE IT'S REALLY HOT OUTSIDE.
YEAH, THE WEATHER IS WEIRD.
IT'S TOO EARLY IN THE YEAR FOR IT TO BE SO HOT.
IT'S CALLED CLIMATE CHANGE.

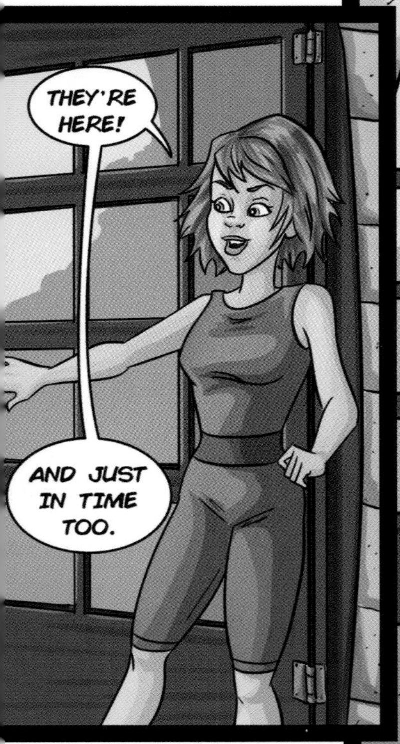
THEY'RE HERE!
AND JUST IN TIME TOO.

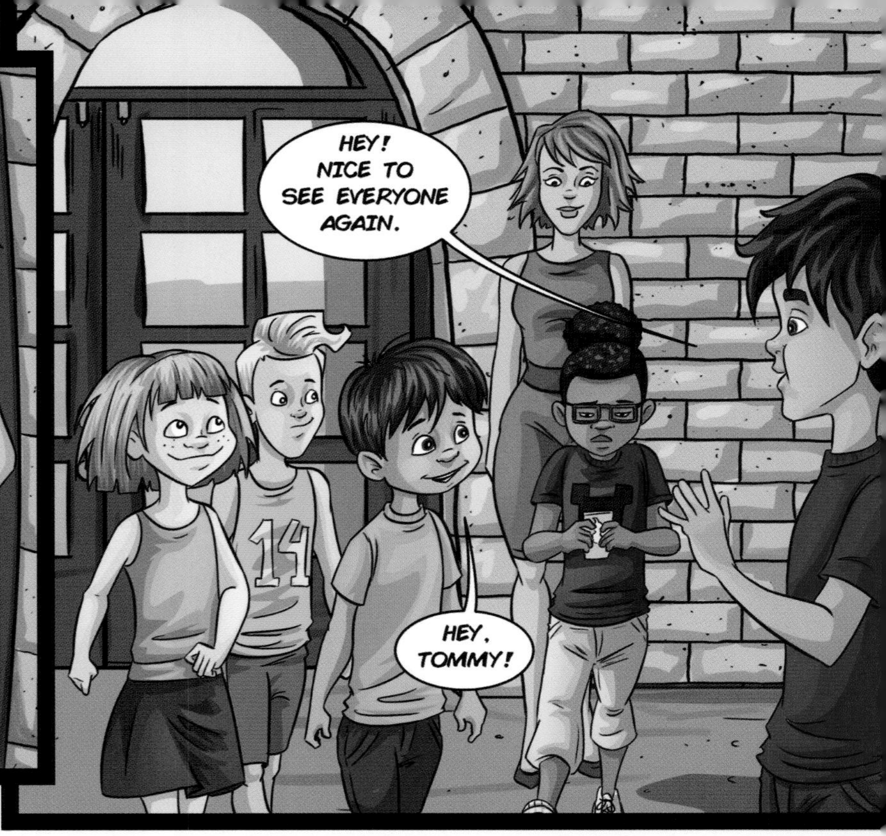
HEY! NICE TO SEE EVERYONE AGAIN.
HEY, TOMMY!

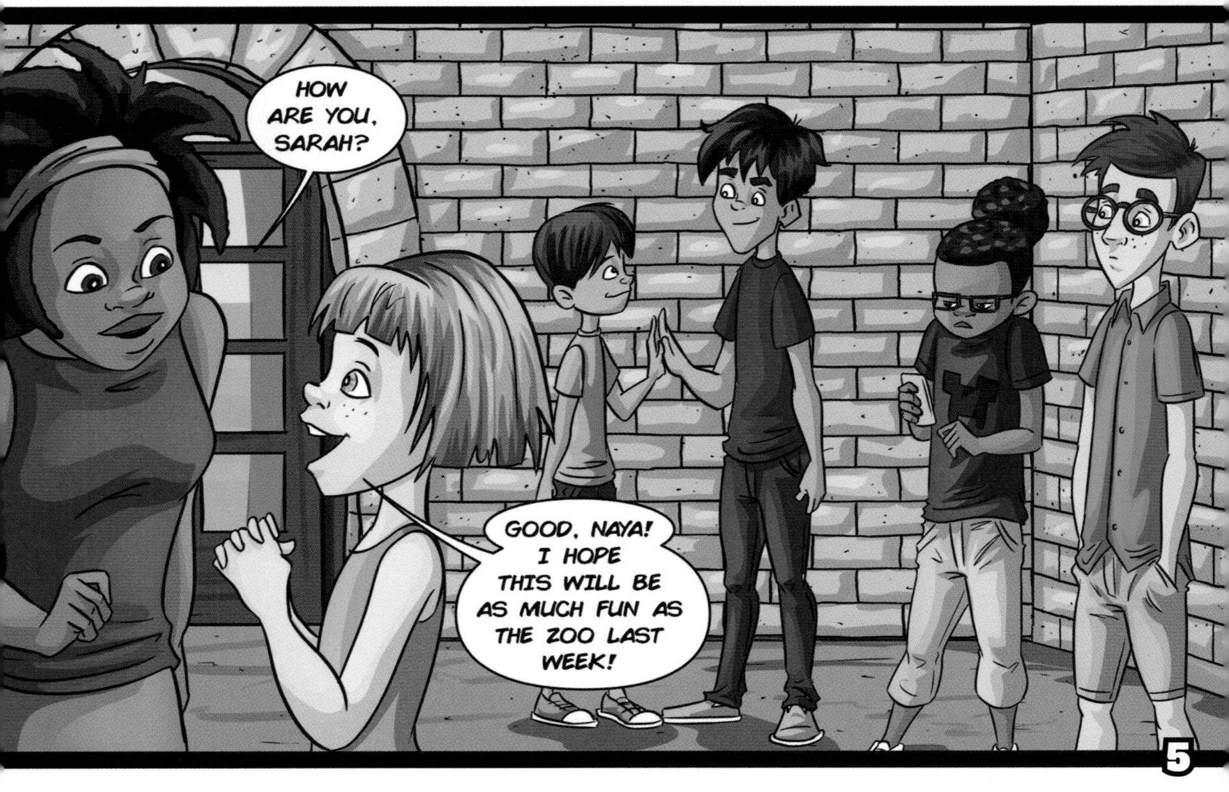
HOW ARE YOU, SARAH?
GOOD, NAYA! I HOPE THIS WILL BE AS MUCH FUN AS THE ZOO LAST WEEK!

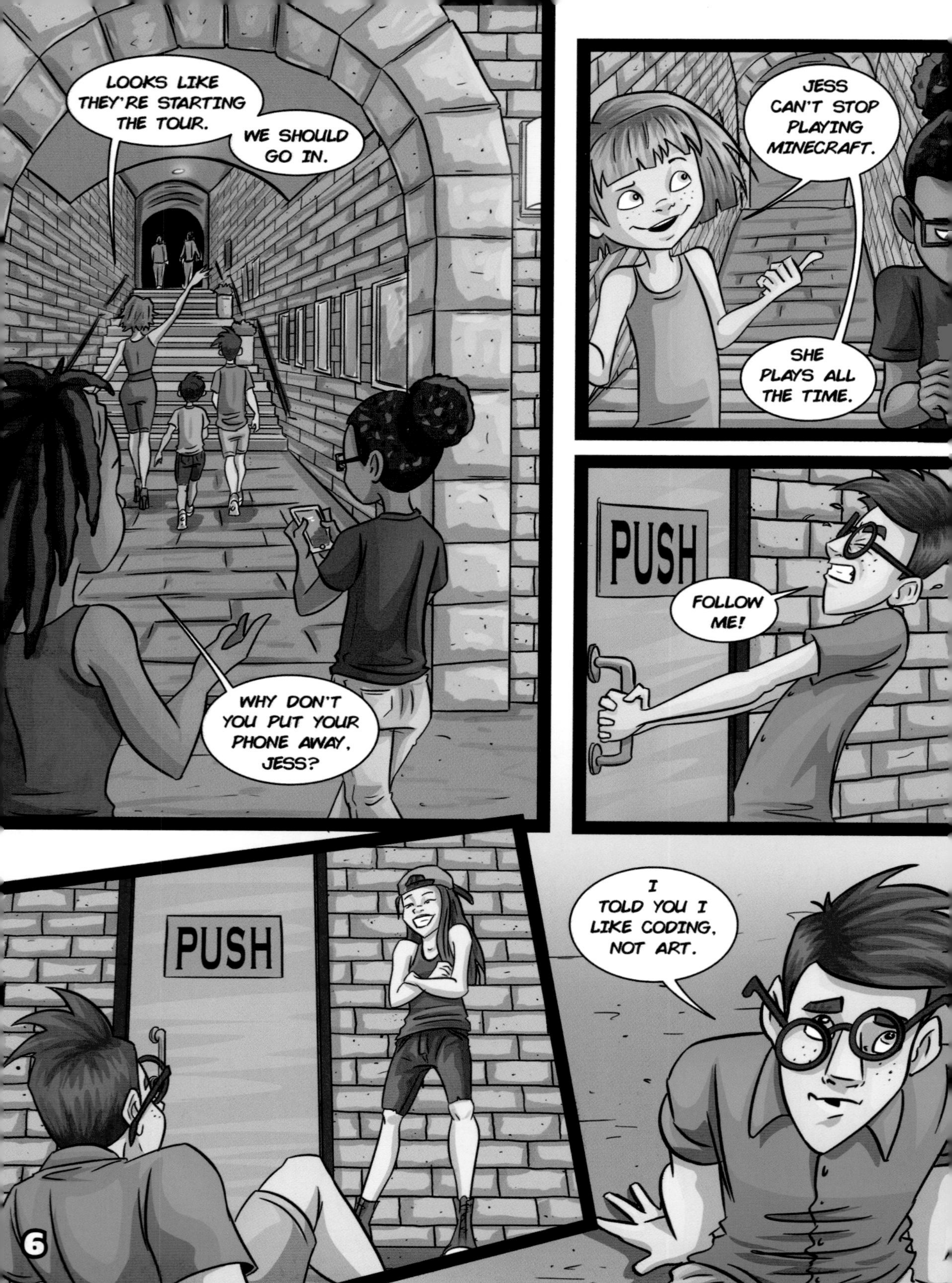
LOOKS LIKE THEY'RE STARTING THE TOUR.
WE SHOULD GO IN.
WHY DON'T YOU PUT YOUR PHONE AWAY, JESS?
JESS CAN'T STOP PLAYING MINECRAFT.
SHE PLAYS ALL THE TIME.
PUSH
FOLLOW ME!
PUSH
I TOLD YOU I LIKE CODING, NOT ART.

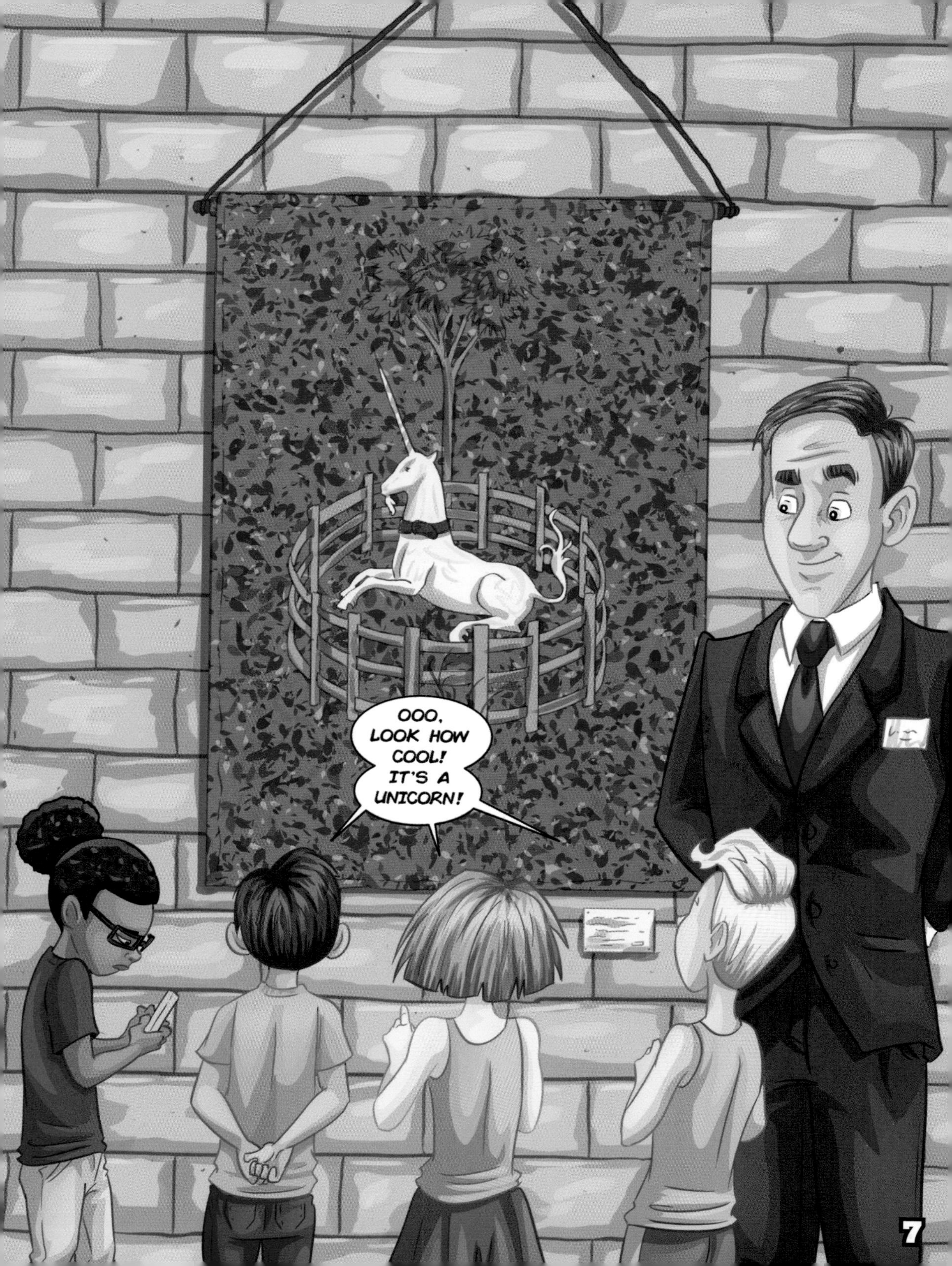
OOO, LOOK HOW COOL! IT'S A UNICORN!

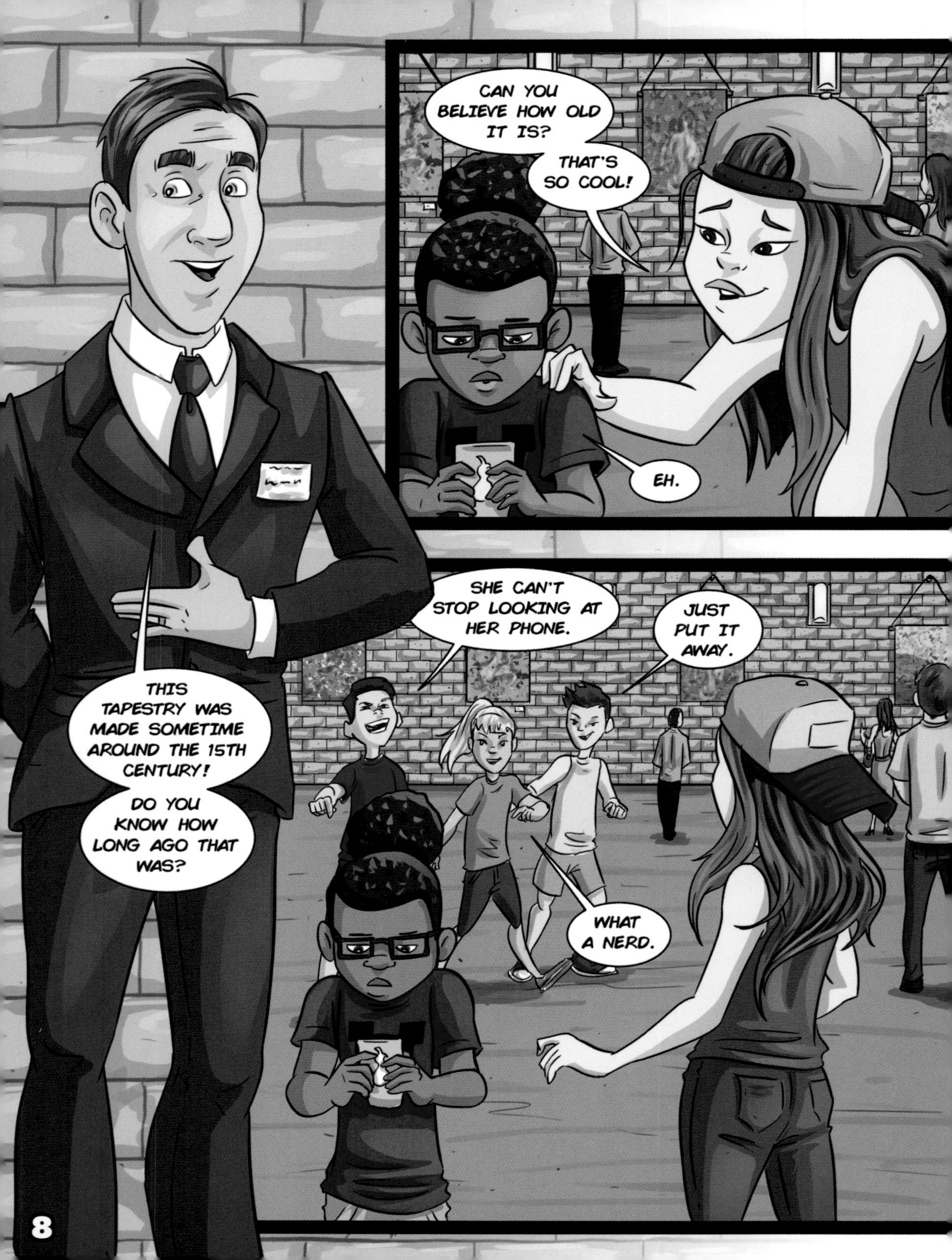
CAN YOU BELIEVE HOW OLD IT IS?
THAT'S SO COOL!
EH.
THIS TAPESTRY WAS MADE SOMETIME AROUND THE 15TH CENTURY!
DO YOU KNOW HOW LONG AGO THAT WAS?
SHE CAN'T STOP LOOKING AT HER PHONE.
JUST PUT IT AWAY.
WHAT A NERD.

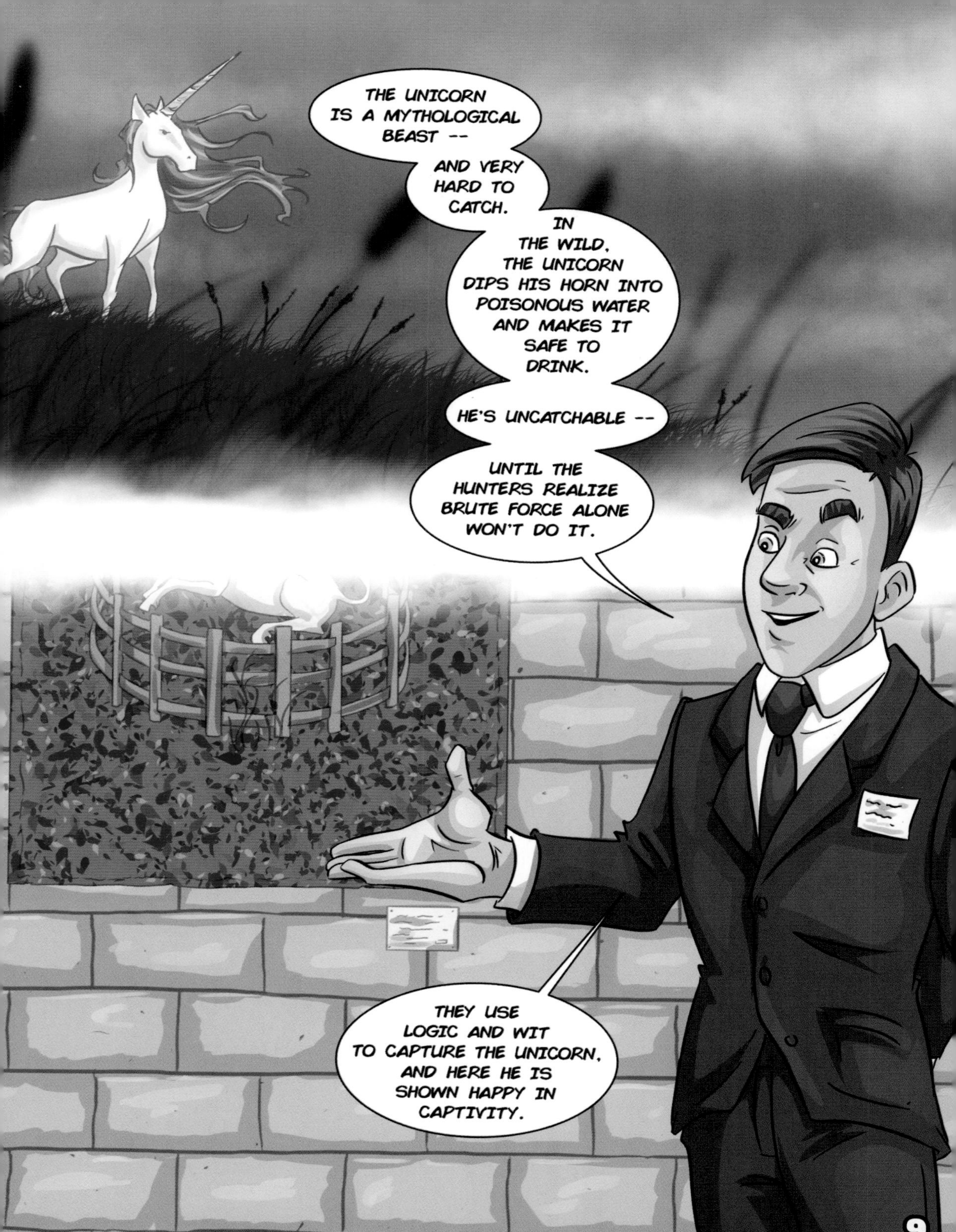
THE UNICORN IS A MYTHOLOGICAL BEAST --
AND VERY HARD TO CATCH.
IN THE WILD, THE UNICORN DIPS HIS HORN INTO POISONOUS WATER AND MAKES IT SAFE TO DRINK.
HE'S UNCATCHABLE --
UNTIL THE HUNTERS REALIZE BRUTE FORCE ALONE WON'T DO IT.
THEY USE LOGIC AND WIT TO CAPTURE THE UNICORN, AND HERE HE IS SHOWN HAPPY IN CAPTIVITY.

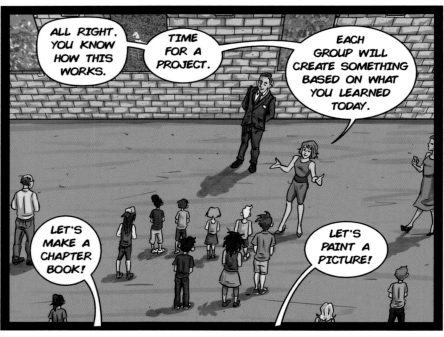

ALL RIGHT. YOU KNOW HOW THIS WORKS.

TIME FOR A PROJECT.

EACH GROUP WILL CREATE SOMETHING BASED ON WHAT YOU LEARNED TODAY.

LET'S MAKE A CHAPTER BOOK!

LET'S PAINT A PICTURE!

DID YOU HEAR HOW THE UNICORN CHANGED THE WATER AND HELPED THE FOREST?

THE UNICORN WAS A SYMBOL OF GOOD THINGS.

I WISH WE HAD A UNICORN TO MAKE OUR ENVIRONMENT BETTER.

MAYBE THAT'S WHAT THE PROJECT SHOULD BE ABOUT.

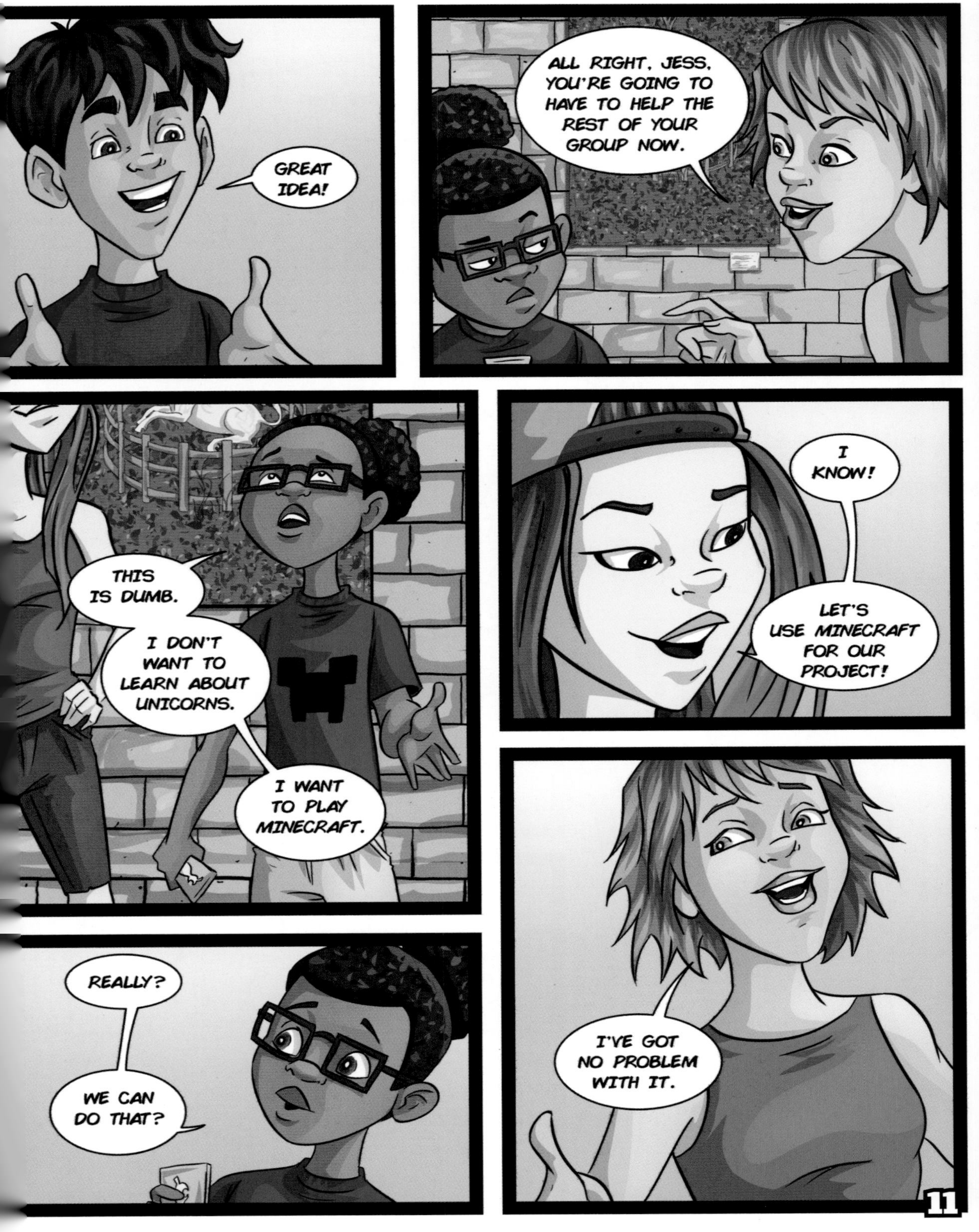
GREAT IDEA!
ALL RIGHT, JESS, YOU'RE GOING TO HAVE TO HELP THE REST OF YOUR GROUP NOW.
THIS IS DUMB.
I DON'T WANT TO LEARN ABOUT UNICORNS.
I WANT TO PLAY MINECRAFT.
I KNOW!
LET'S USE MINECRAFT FOR OUR PROJECT!
REALLY?
WE CAN DO THAT?
I'VE GOT NO PROBLEM WITH IT.

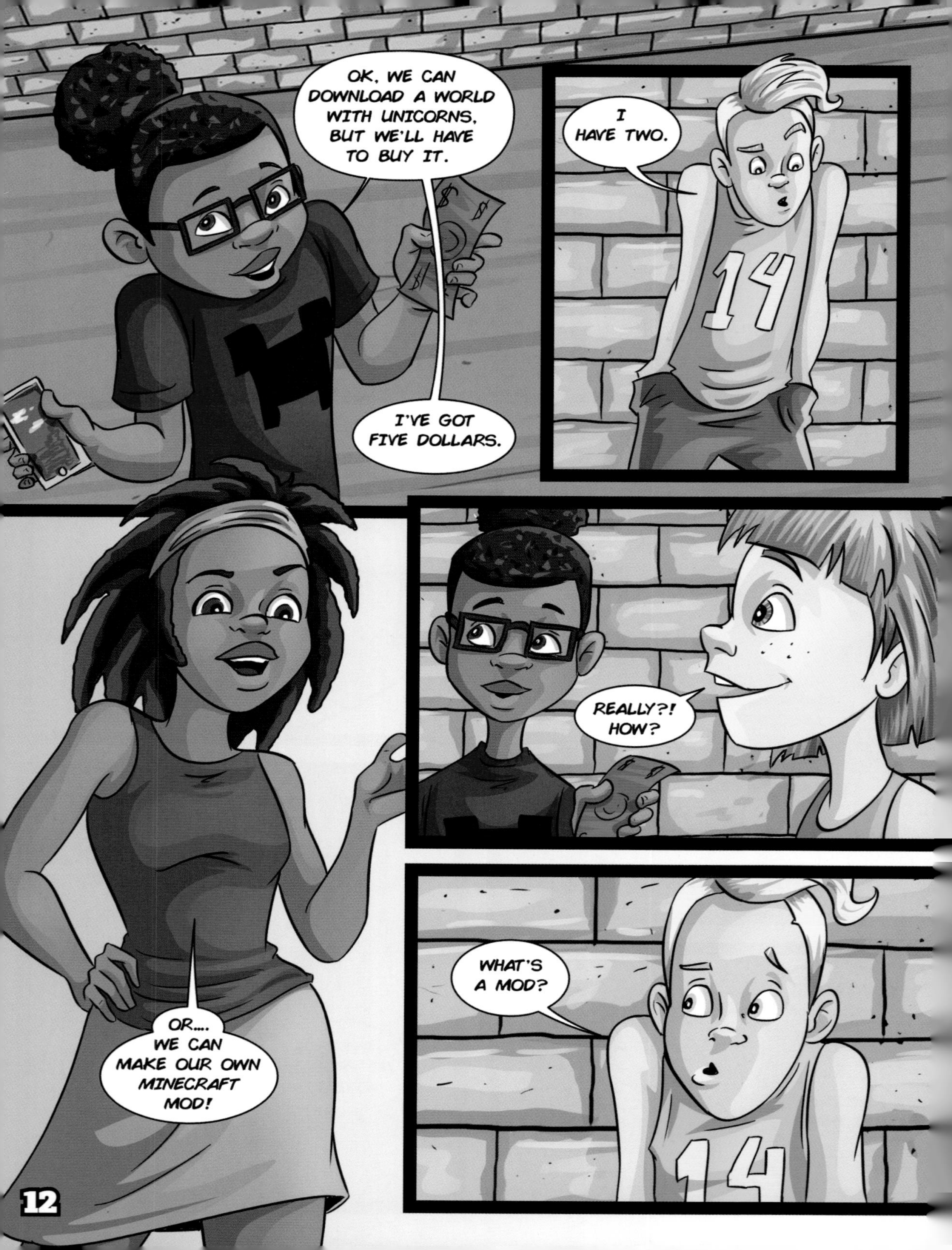

OK, WE CAN DOWNLOAD A WORLD WITH UNICORNS, BUT WE'LL HAVE TO BUY IT.
I'VE GOT FIVE DOLLARS.
I HAVE TWO.
OR.... WE CAN MAKE OUR OWN MINECRAFT MOD!
REALLY?! HOW?
WHAT'S A MOD?

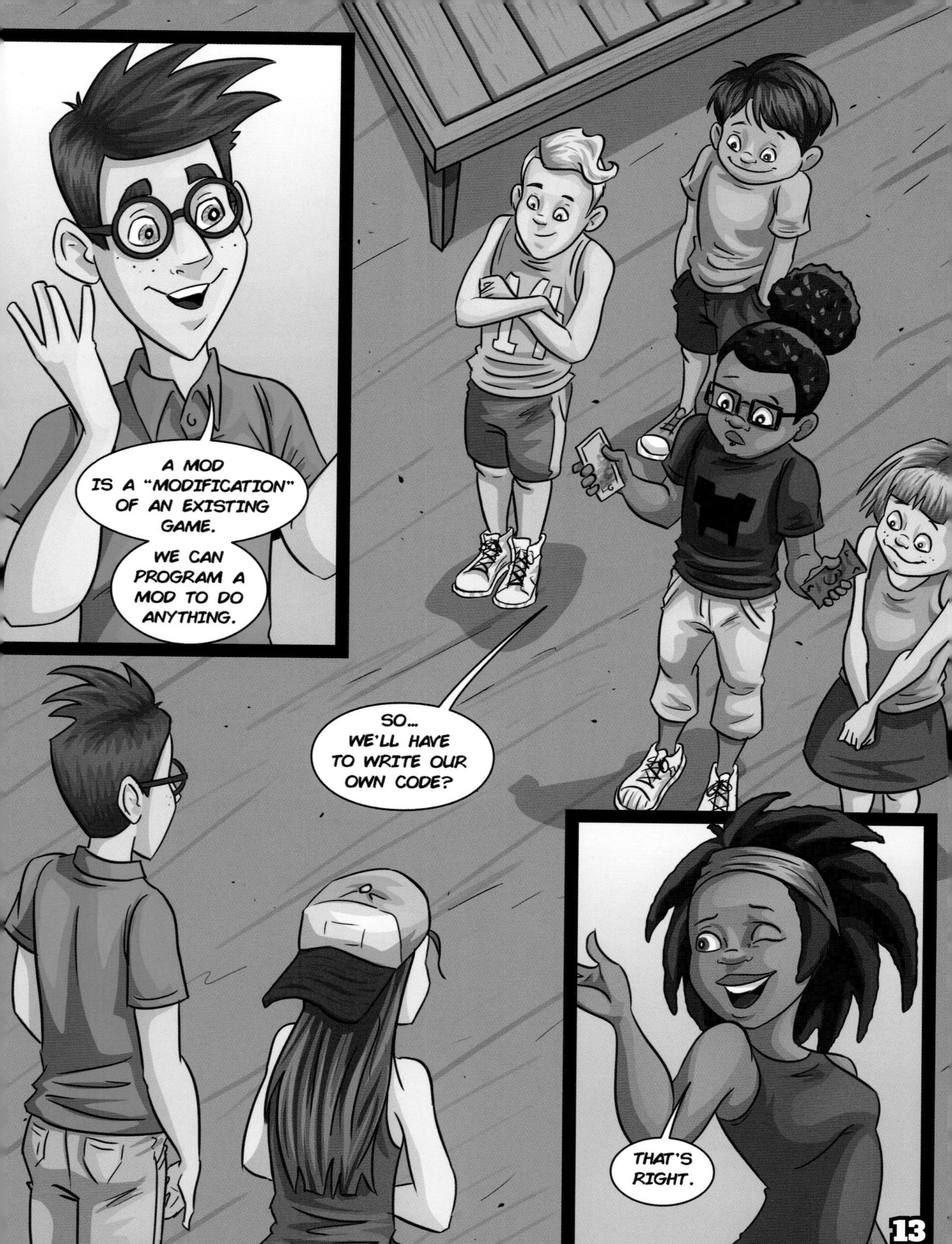
A MOD IS A "MODIFICATION" OF AN EXISTING GAME.
WE CAN PROGRAM A MOD TO DO ANYTHING.
SO... WE'LL HAVE TO WRITE OUR OWN CODE?
THAT'S RIGHT.

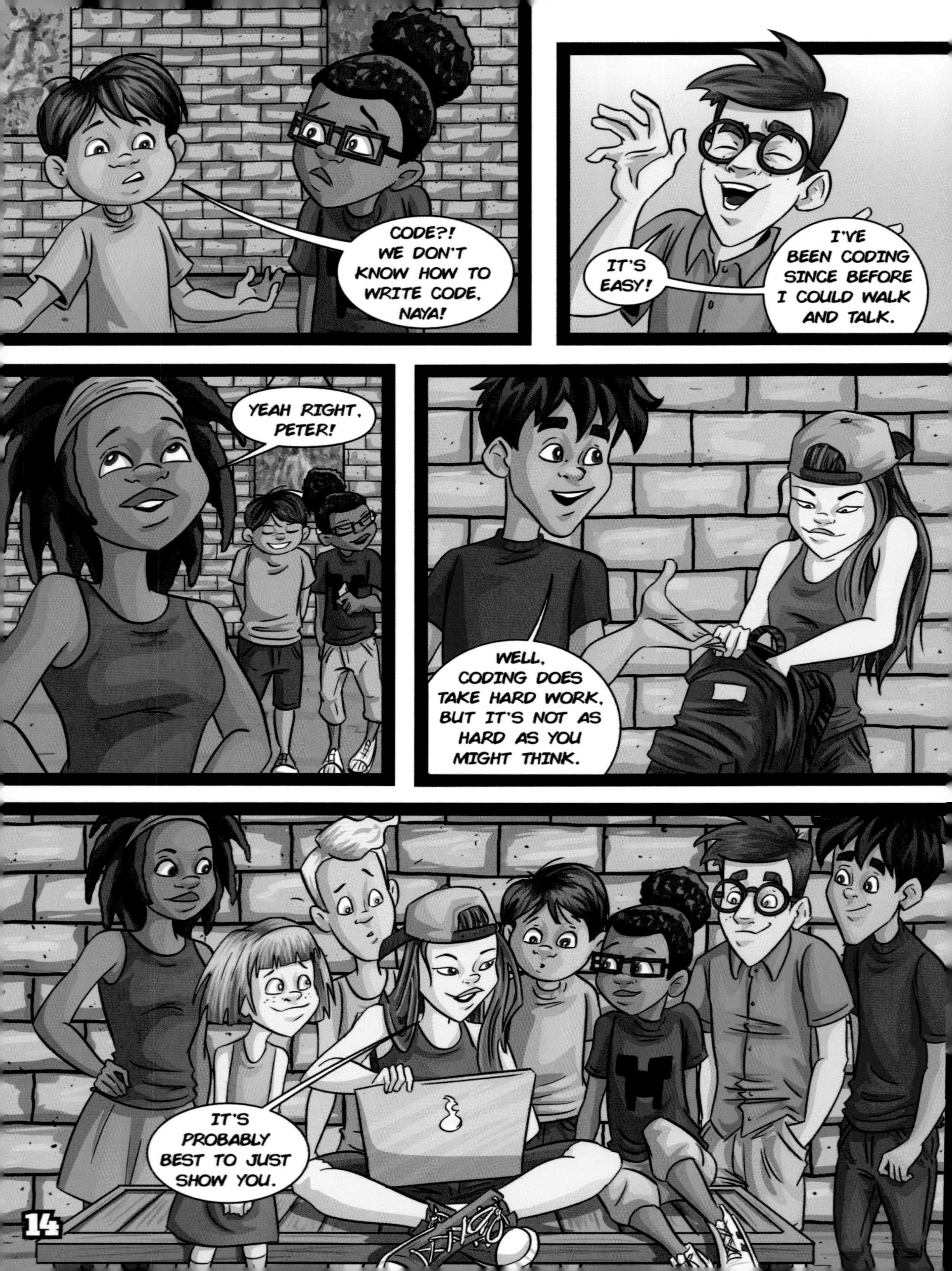

CODE?! WE DON'T KNOW HOW TO WRITE CODE, NAYA!
IT'S EASY!
I'VE BEEN CODING SINCE BEFORE I COULD WALK AND TALK.
YEAH RIGHT, PETER!
WELL, CODING DOES TAKE HARD WORK, BUT IT'S NOT AS HARD AS YOU MIGHT THINK.
IT'S PROBABLY BEST TO JUST SHOW YOU.

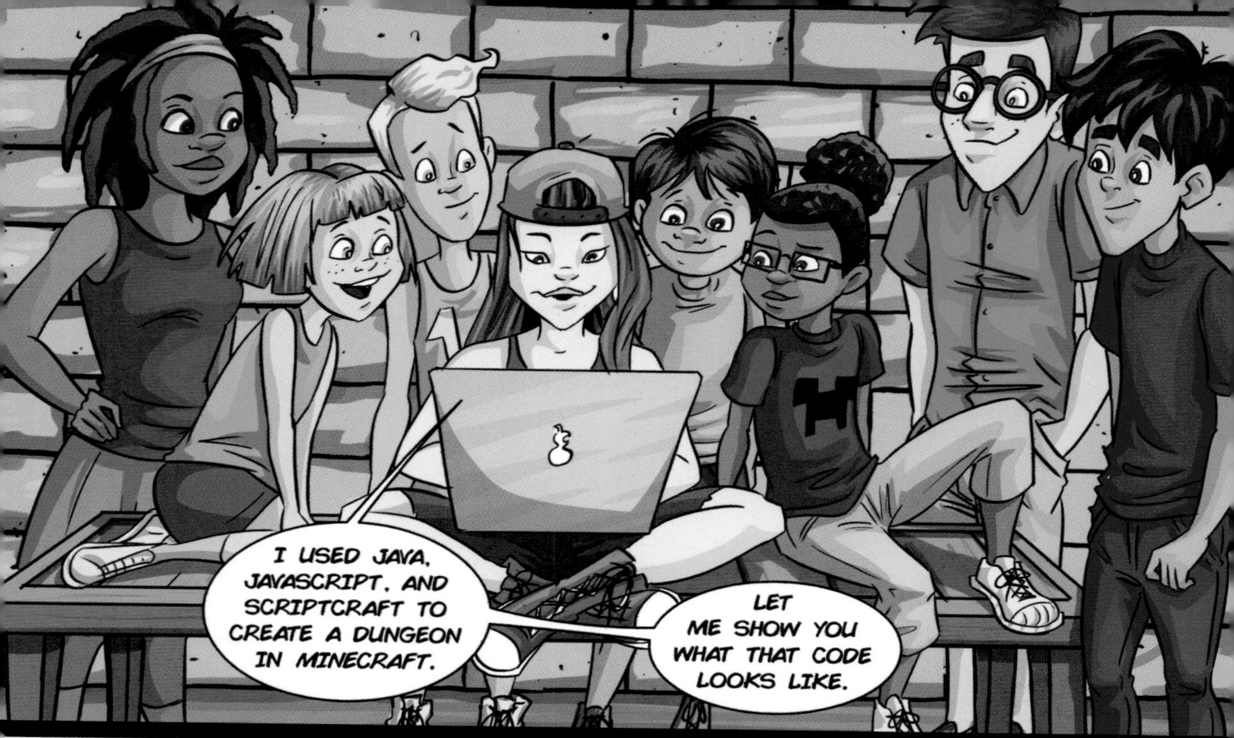
I USED JAVA, JAVASCRIPT, AND SCRIPTCRAFT TO CREATE A DUNGEON IN MINECRAFT.
LET ME SHOW YOU WHAT THAT CODE LOOKS LIKE.

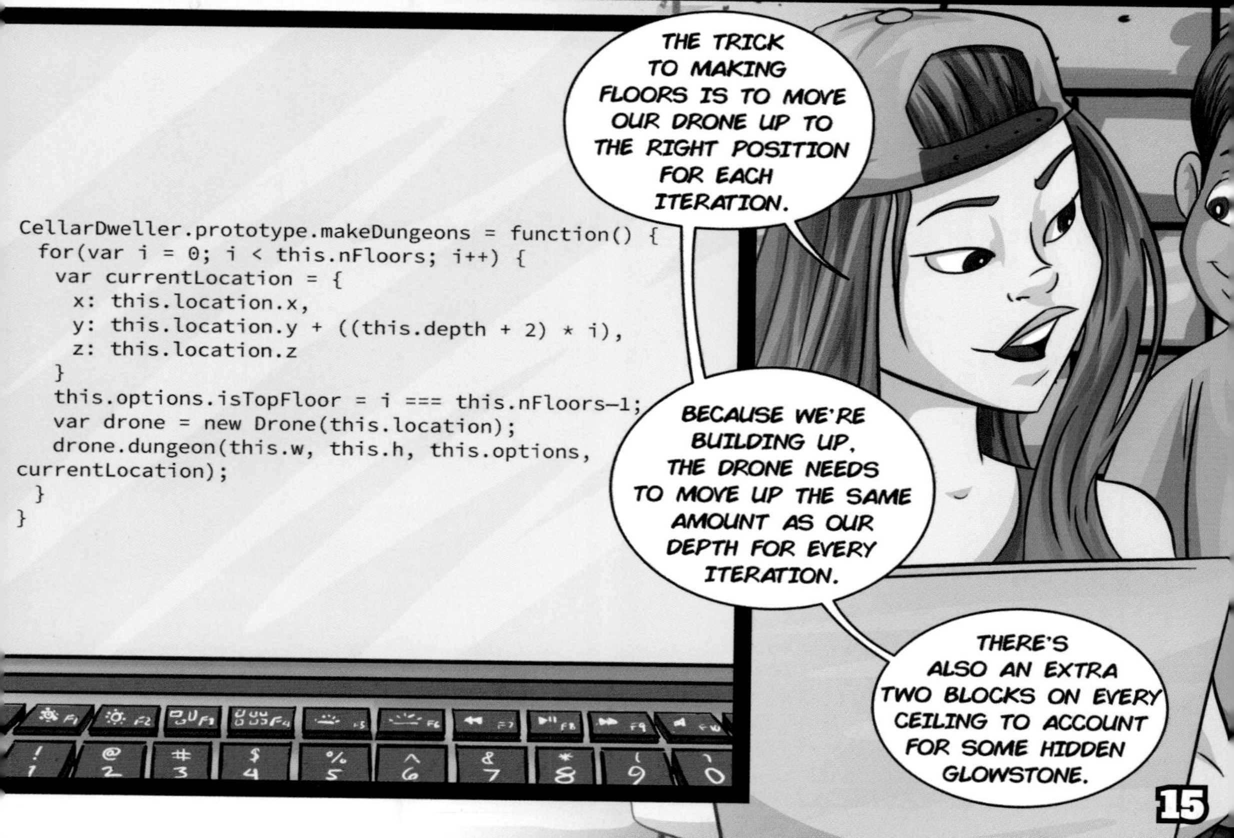
THE TRICK TO MAKING FLOORS IS TO MOVE OUR DRONE UP TO THE RIGHT POSITION FOR EACH ITERATION.
BECAUSE WE'RE BUILDING UP, THE DRONE NEEDS TO MOVE UP THE SAME AMOUNT AS OUR DEPTH FOR EVERY ITERATION.
THERE'S ALSO AN EXTRA TWO BLOCKS ON EVERY CEILING TO ACCOUNT FOR SOME HIDDEN GLOWSTONE.

```
CellarDweller.prototype.makeDungeons = function() {
  for(var i = 0; i < this.nFloors; i++) {
    var currentLocation = {
      x: this.location.x,
      y: this.location.y + ((this.depth + 2) * i),
      z: this.location.z
    }
    this.options.isTopFloor = i === this.nFloors-1;
    var drone = new Drone(this.location);
    drone.dungeon(this.w, this.h, this.options,
currentLocation);
  }
}
```

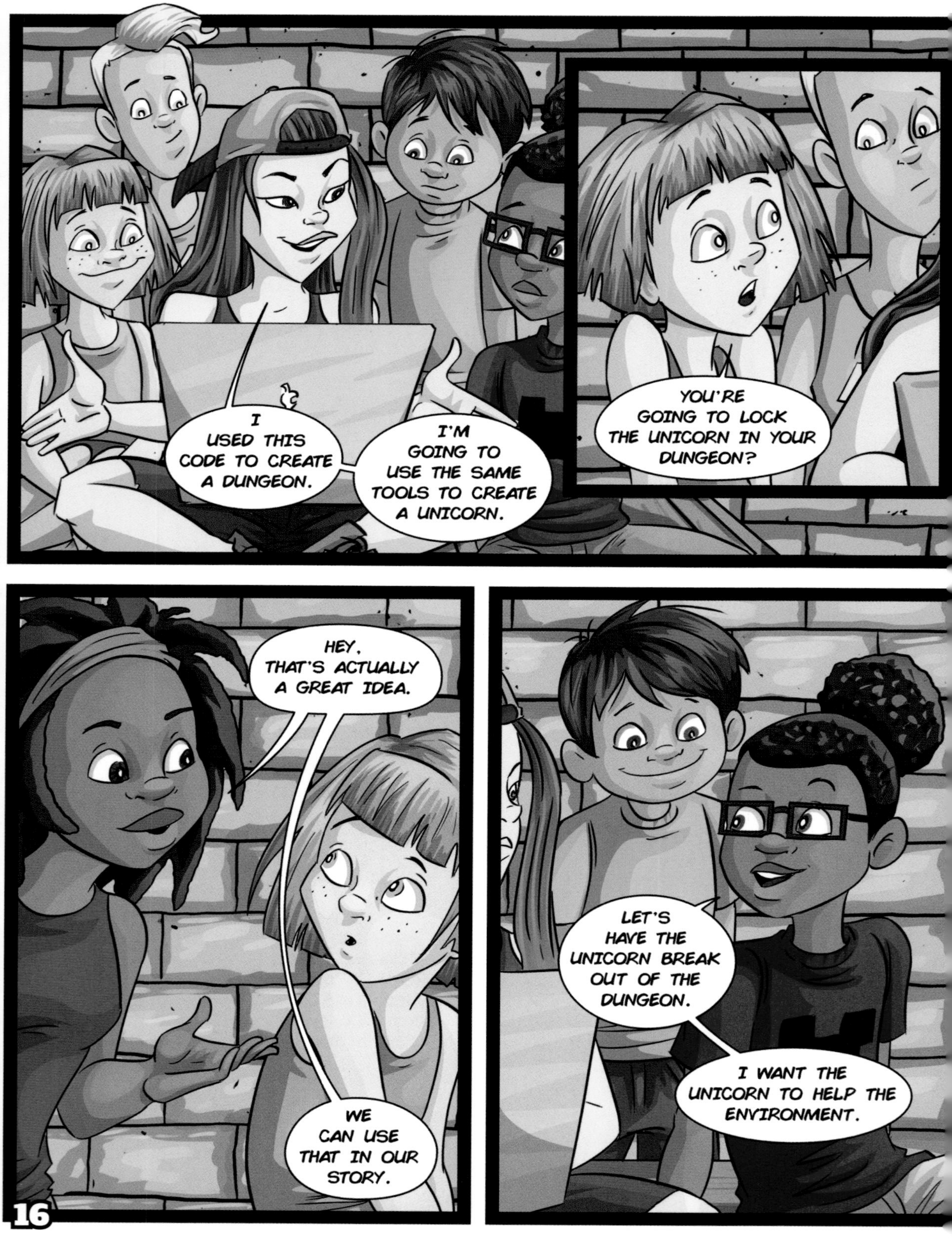
I USED THIS CODE TO CREATE A DUNGEON.
I'M GOING TO USE THE SAME TOOLS TO CREATE A UNICORN.
YOU'RE GOING TO LOCK THE UNICORN IN YOUR DUNGEON?
HEY, THAT'S ACTUALLY A GREAT IDEA.
WE CAN USE THAT IN OUR STORY.
LET'S HAVE THE UNICORN BREAK OUT OF THE DUNGEON.
I WANT THE UNICORN TO HELP THE ENVIRONMENT.

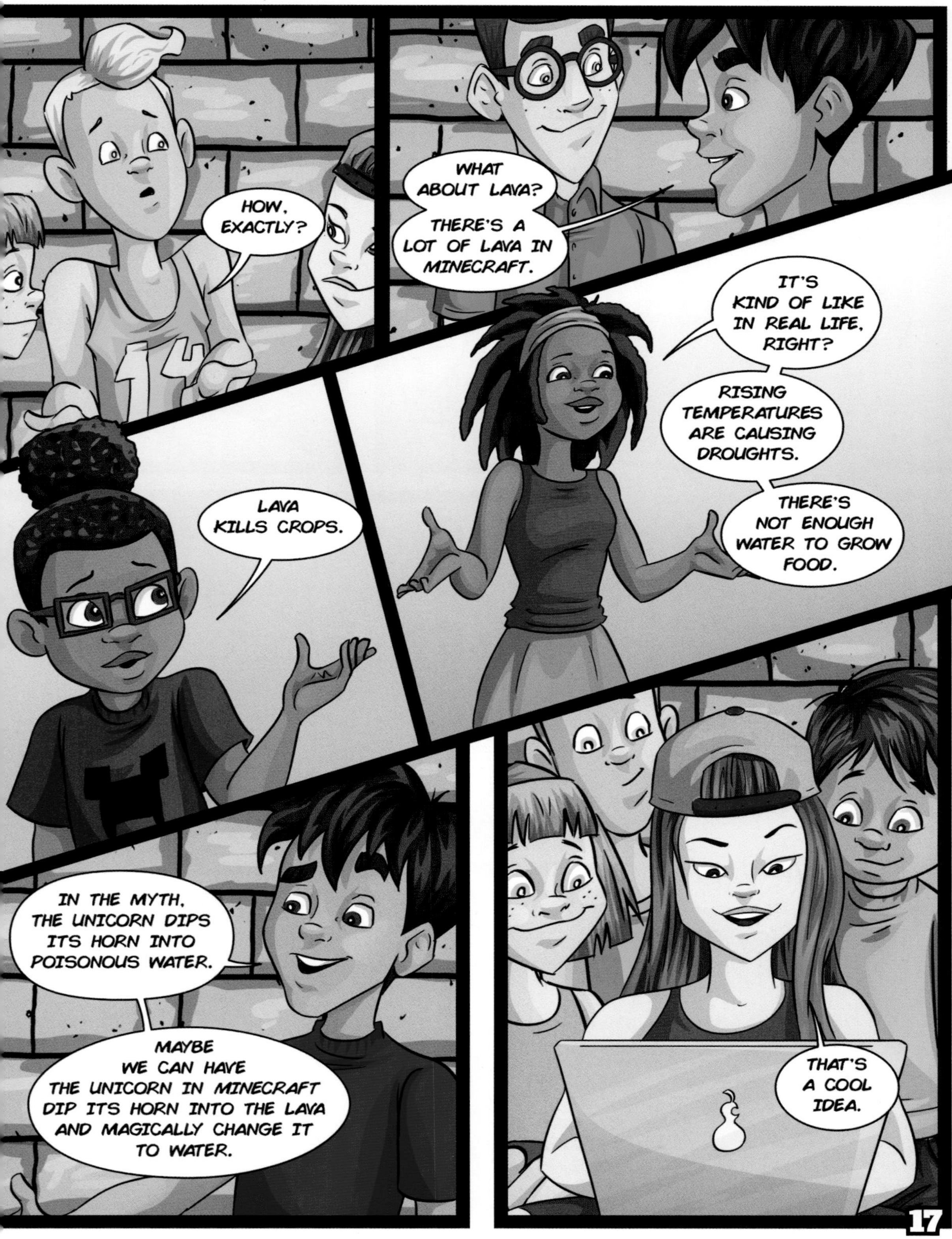
HOW, EXACTLY?
WHAT ABOUT LAVA?
THERE'S A LOT OF LAVA IN MINECRAFT.
IT'S KIND OF LIKE IN REAL LIFE, RIGHT?
RISING TEMPERATURES ARE CAUSING DROUGHTS.
THERE'S NOT ENOUGH WATER TO GROW FOOD.
LAVA KILLS CROPS.
IN THE MYTH, THE UNICORN DIPS ITS HORN INTO POISONOUS WATER.
MAYBE WE CAN HAVE THE UNICORN IN MINECRAFT DIP ITS HORN INTO THE LAVA AND MAGICALLY CHANGE IT TO WATER.
THAT'S A COOL IDEA.

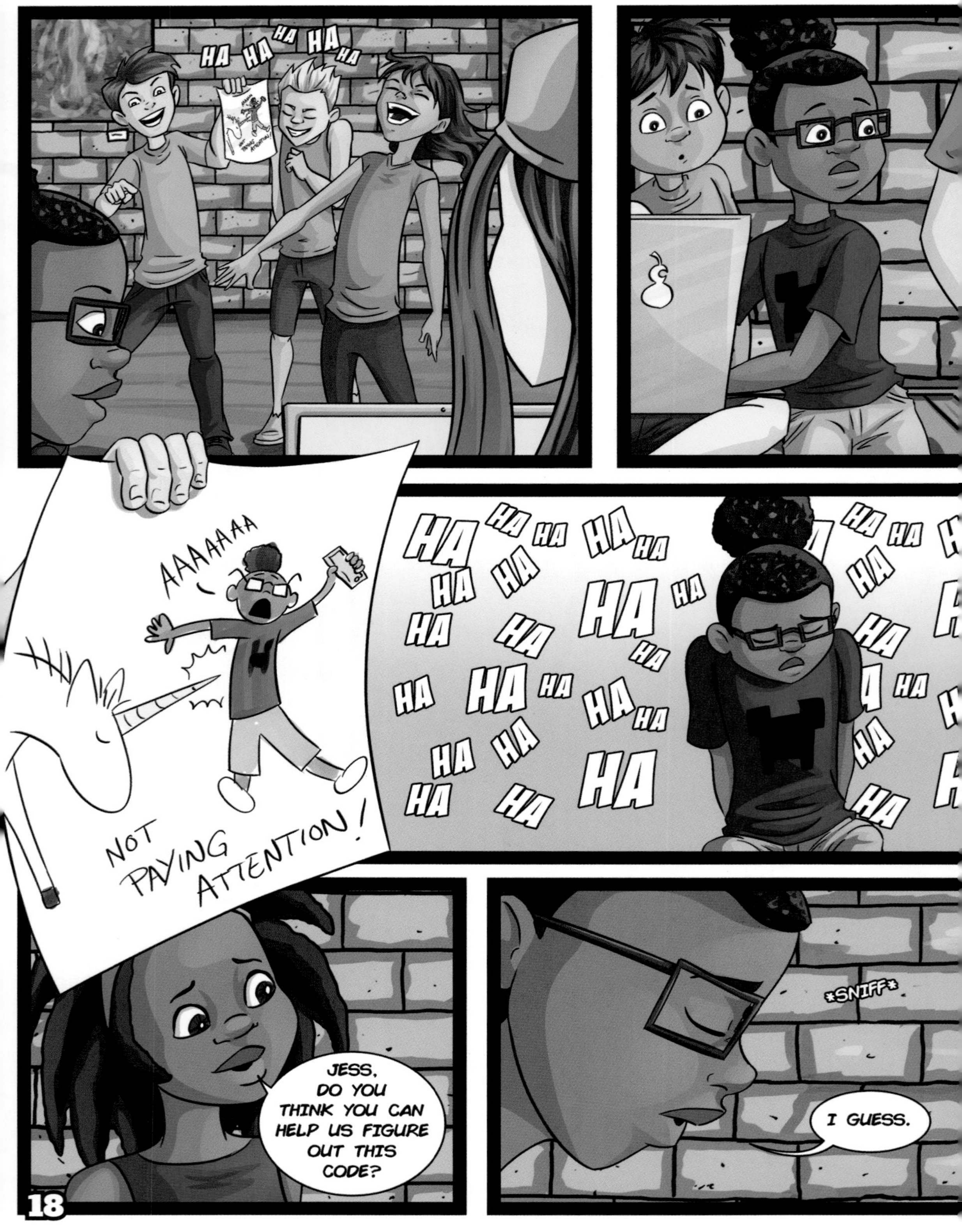
HA HA HA HA HA
AAAAAAA
NOT PAYING ATTENTION!
HA HA HA HA HA HA HA HA HA HA HA HA HA HA HA HA HA HA HA HA HA HA HA HA HA
JESS, DO YOU THINK YOU CAN HELP US FIGURE OUT THIS CODE?
SNIFF
I GUESS.

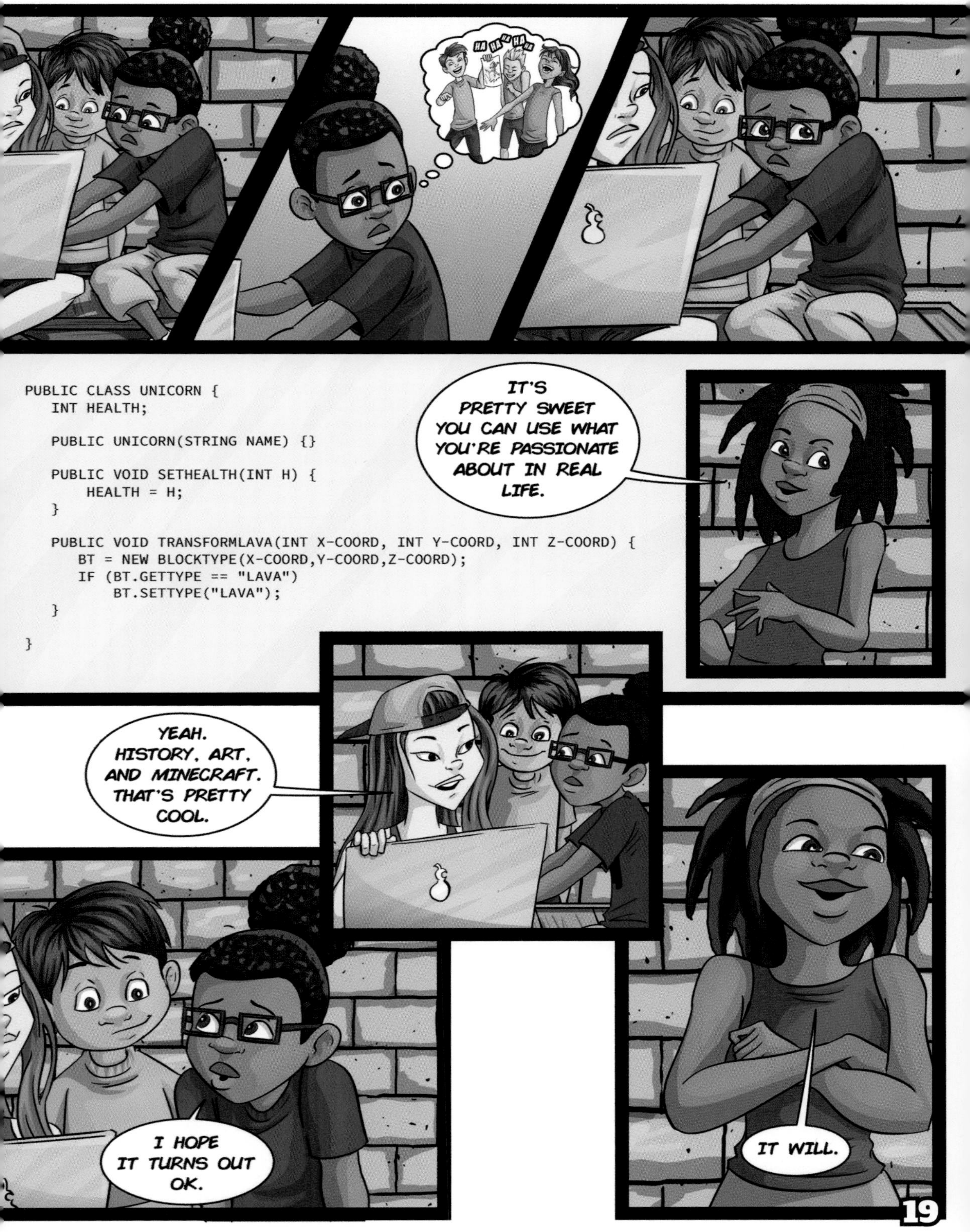
PUBLIC CLASS UNICORN {
INT HEALTH;
PUBLIC UNICORN(STRING NAME) {}
PUBLIC VOID SETHEALTH(INT H) {
HEALTH = H;
}
PUBLIC VOID TRANSFORMLAVA(INT X-COORD, INT Y-COORD, INT Z-COORD) {
BT = NEW BLOCKTYPE(X-COORD,Y-COORD,Z-COORD);
IF (BT.GETTYPE == "LAVA")
BT.SETTYPE("LAVA");
}
}
IT'S PRETTY SWEET YOU CAN USE WHAT YOU'RE PASSIONATE ABOUT IN REAL LIFE.
YEAH. HISTORY, ART, AND MINECRAFT. THAT'S PRETTY COOL.
I HOPE IT TURNS OUT OK.
IT WILL.

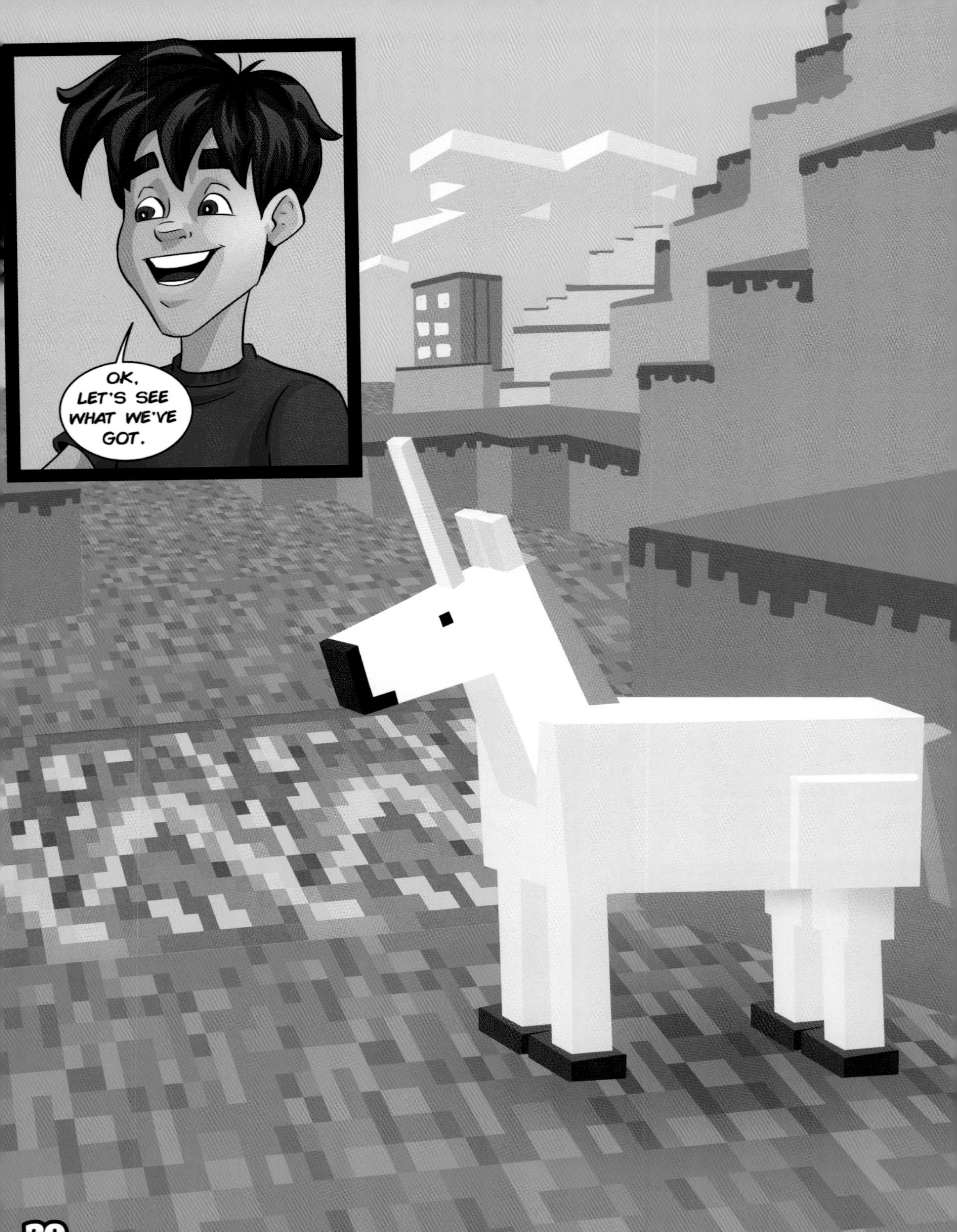
OK, LET'S SEE WHAT WE'VE GOT.

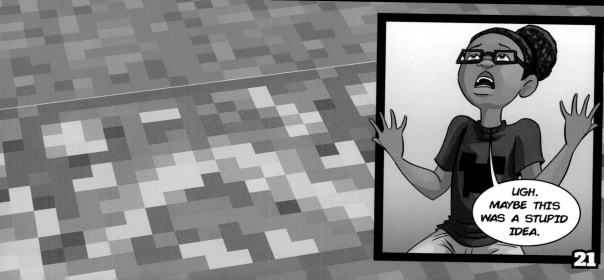

UGH.
MAYBE THIS
WAS A STUPID
IDEA.

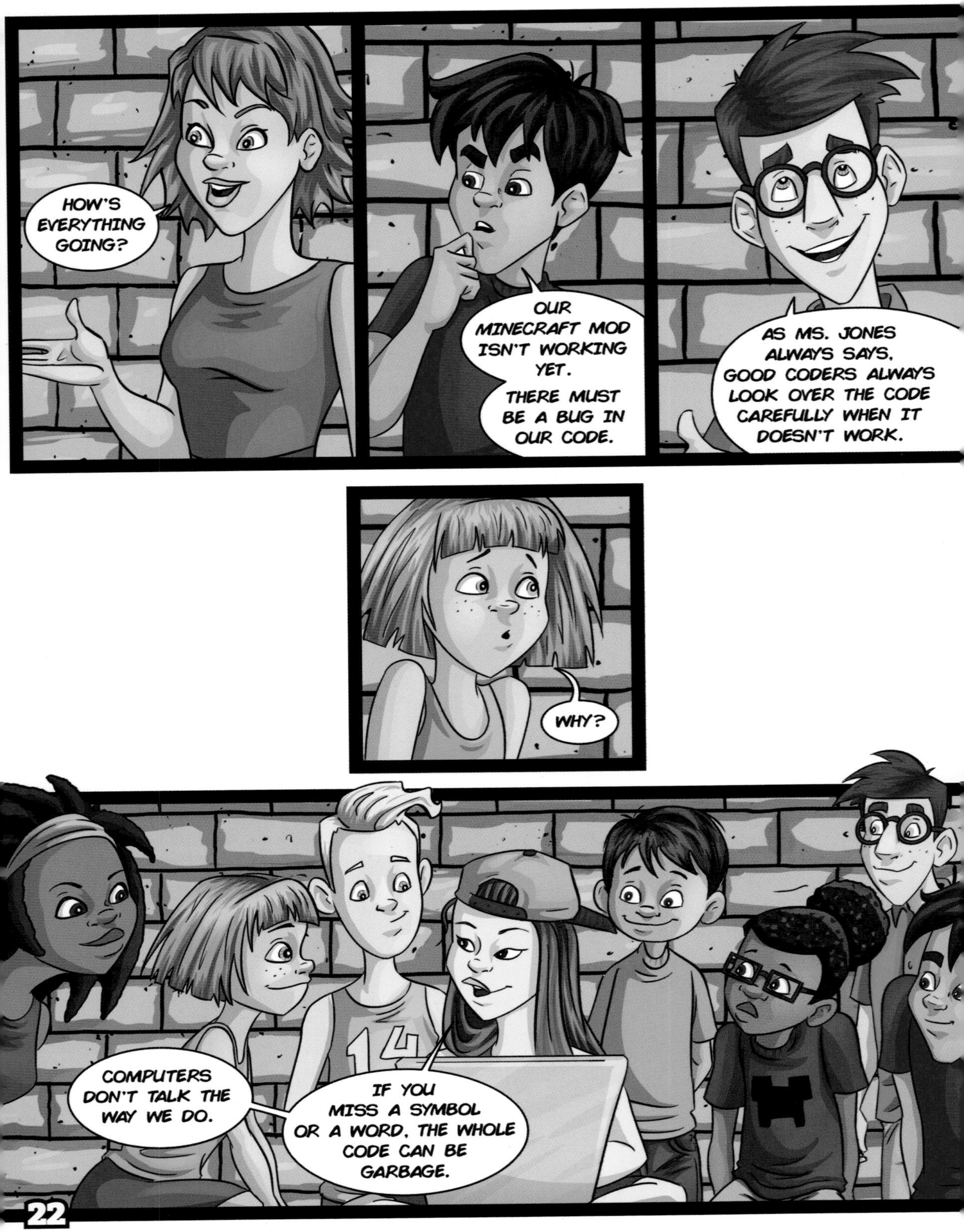
HOW'S EVERYTHING GOING?
OUR MINECRAFT MOD ISN'T WORKING YET.
THERE MUST BE A BUG IN OUR CODE.
AS MS. JONES ALWAYS SAYS, GOOD CODERS ALWAYS LOOK OVER THE CODE CAREFULLY WHEN IT DOESN'T WORK.
WHY?
COMPUTERS DON'T TALK THE WAY WE DO.
IF YOU MISS A SYMBOL OR A WORD, THE WHOLE CODE CAN BE GARBAGE.

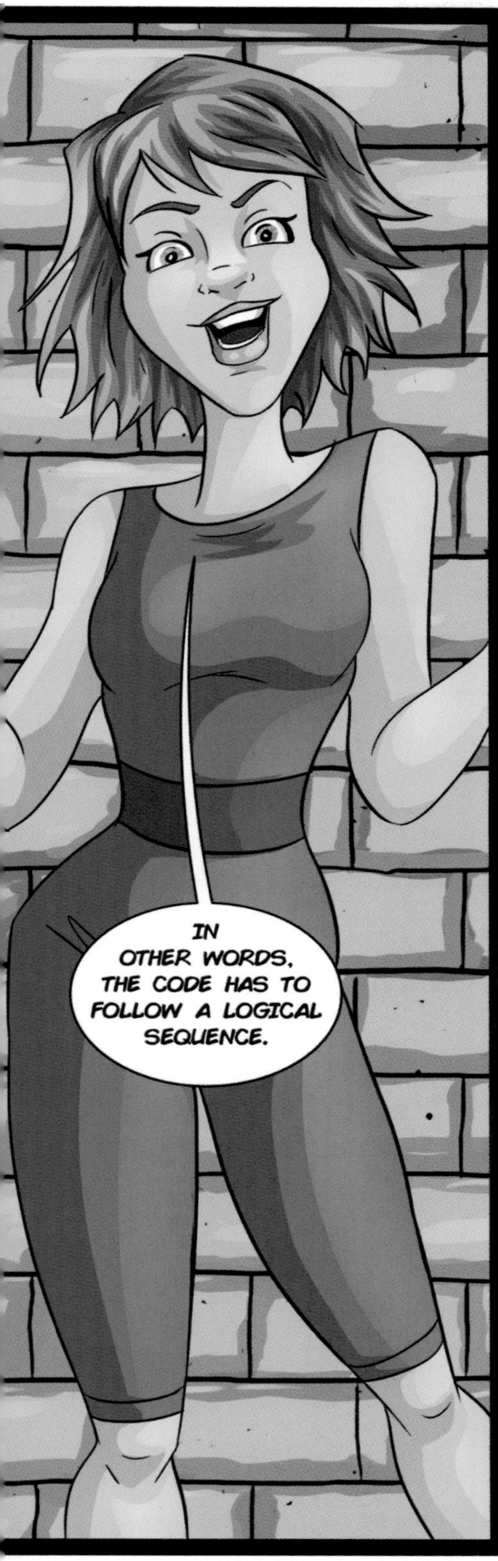
IN OTHER WORDS, THE CODE HAS TO FOLLOW A LOGICAL SEQUENCE.

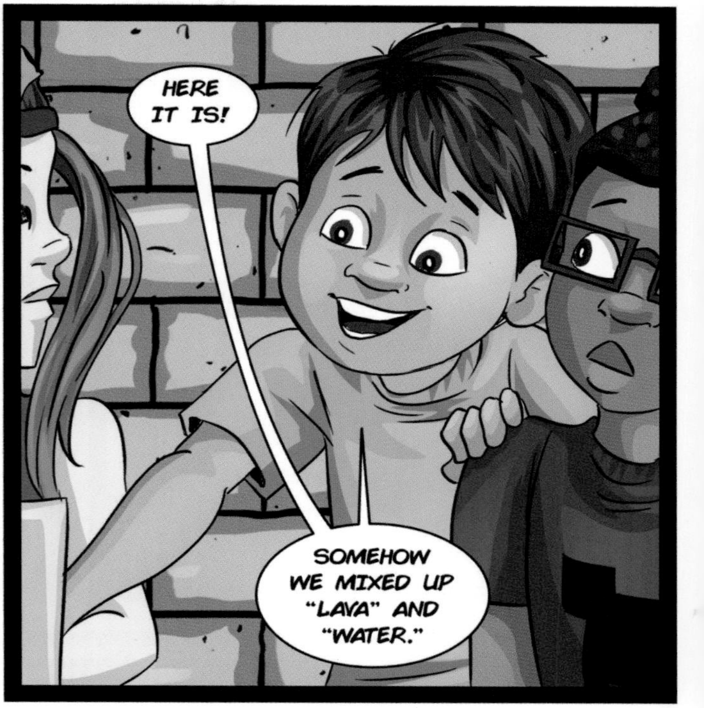
HERE IT IS!
SOMEHOW WE MIXED UP "LAVA" AND "WATER."

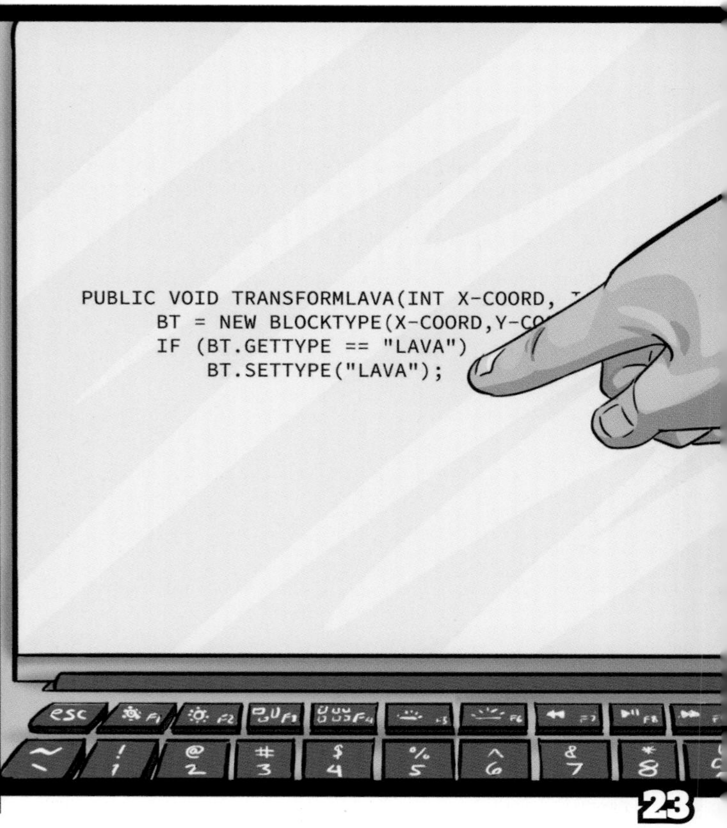
PUBLIC VOID TRANSFORMLAVA(INT X-COORD,
BT = NEW BLOCKTYPE(X-COORD,Y-
IF (BT.GETTYPE == "LAVA")
BT.SETTYPE("LAVA");

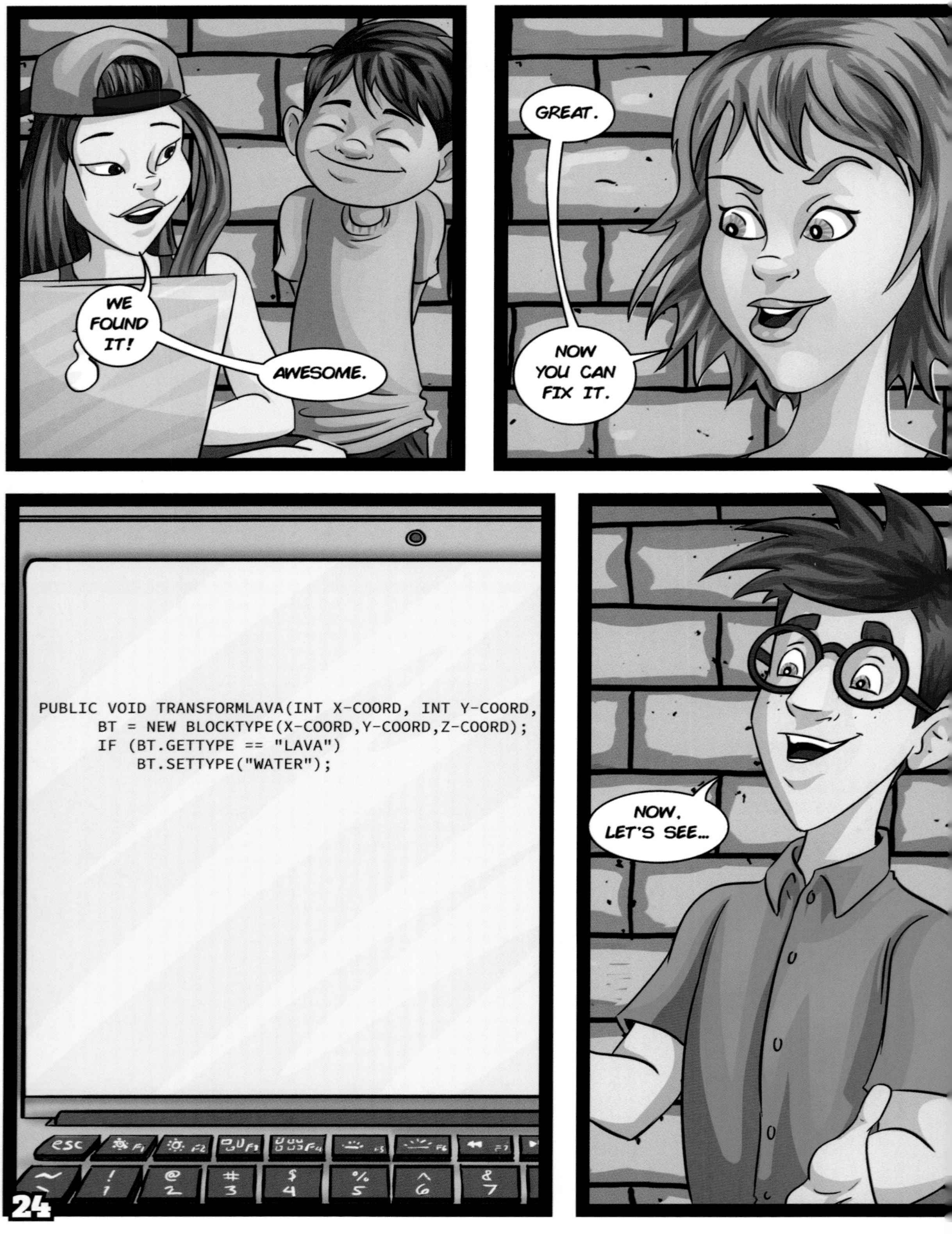
WE FOUND IT!
AWESOME.
GREAT.
NOW YOU CAN FIX IT.
PUBLIC VOID TRANSFORMLAVA(INT X-COORD, INT Y-COORD,
BT = NEW BLOCKTYPE(X-COORD,Y-COORD,Z-COORD);
IF (BT.GETTYPE == "LAVA")
BT.SETTYPE("WATER");
NOW, LET'S SEE...

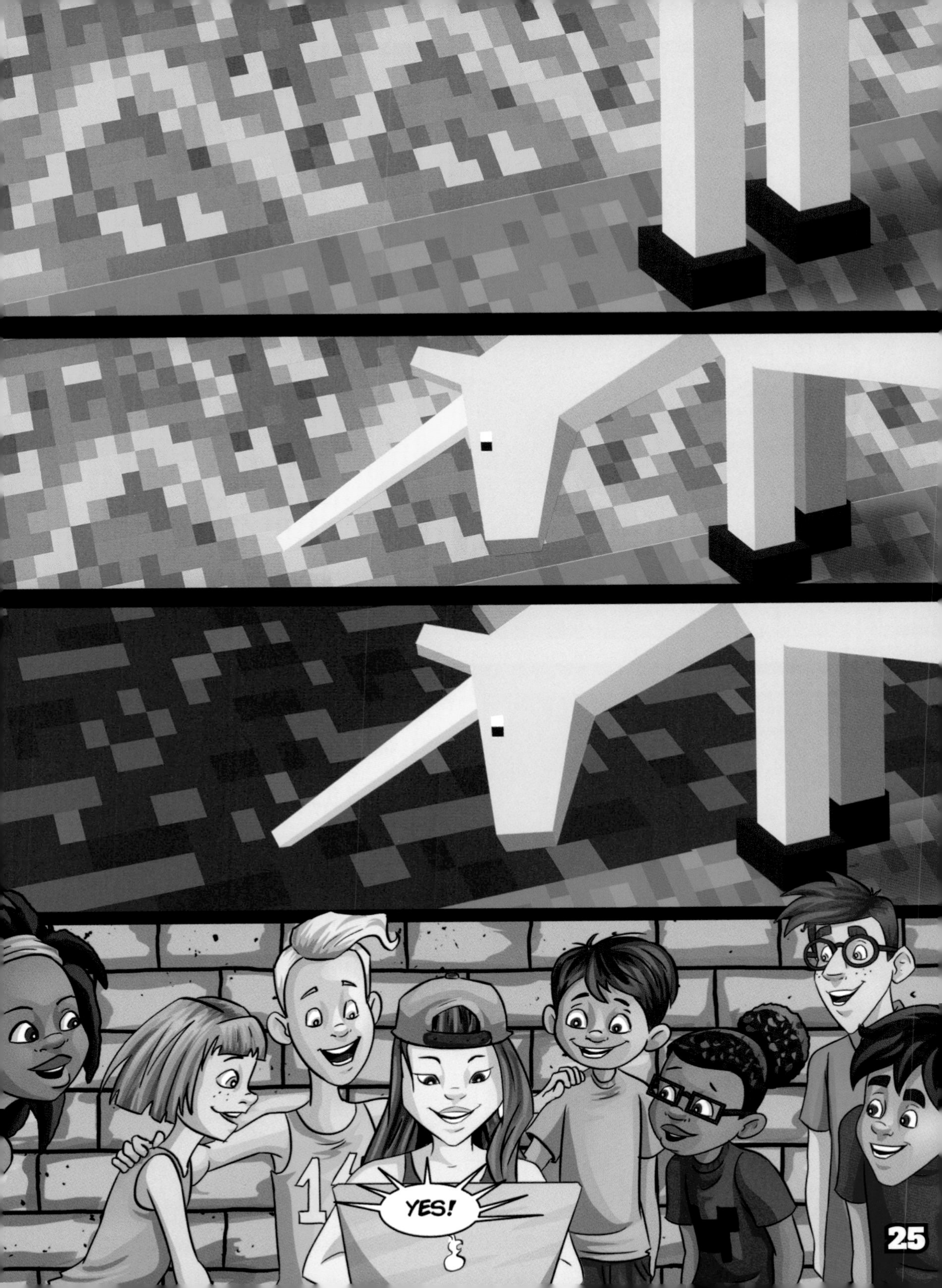
YES!

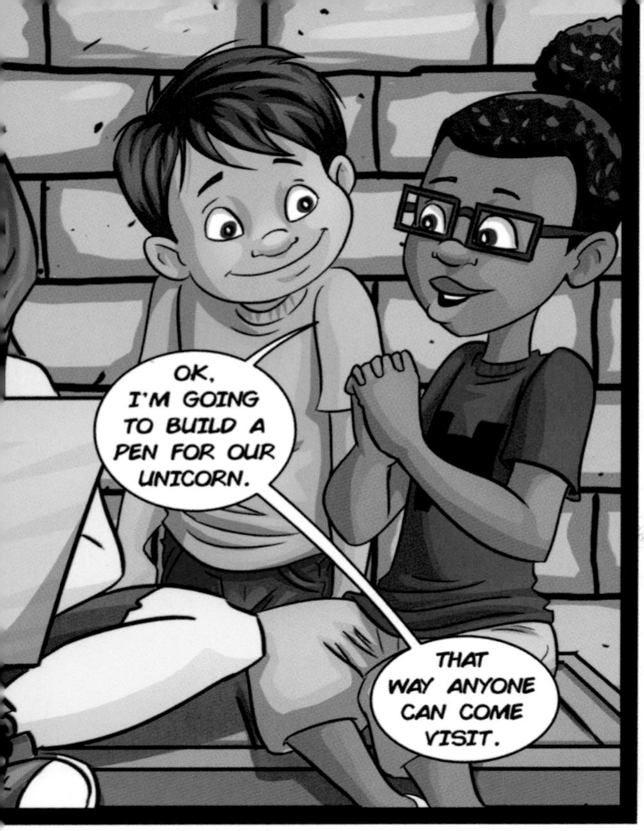
OK, I'M GOING TO BUILD A PEN FOR OUR UNICORN.
THAT WAY ANYONE CAN COME VISIT.

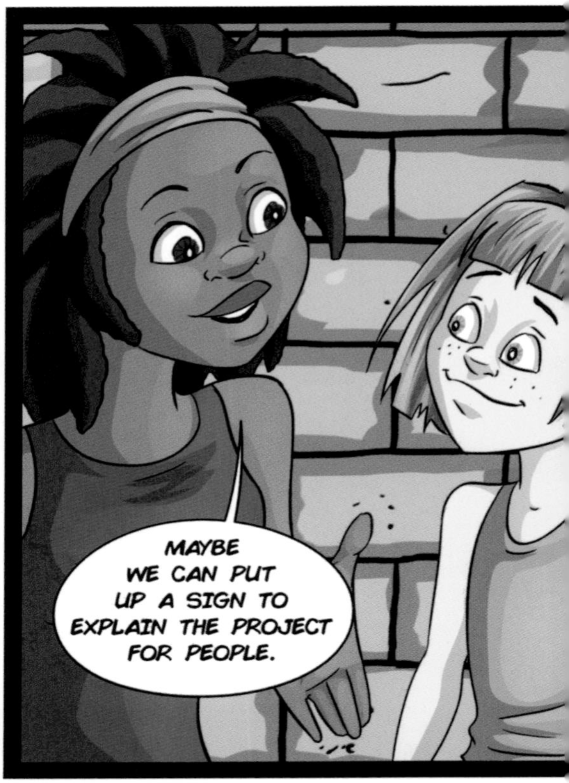
MAYBE WE CAN PUT UP A SIGN TO EXPLAIN THE PROJECT FOR PEOPLE.

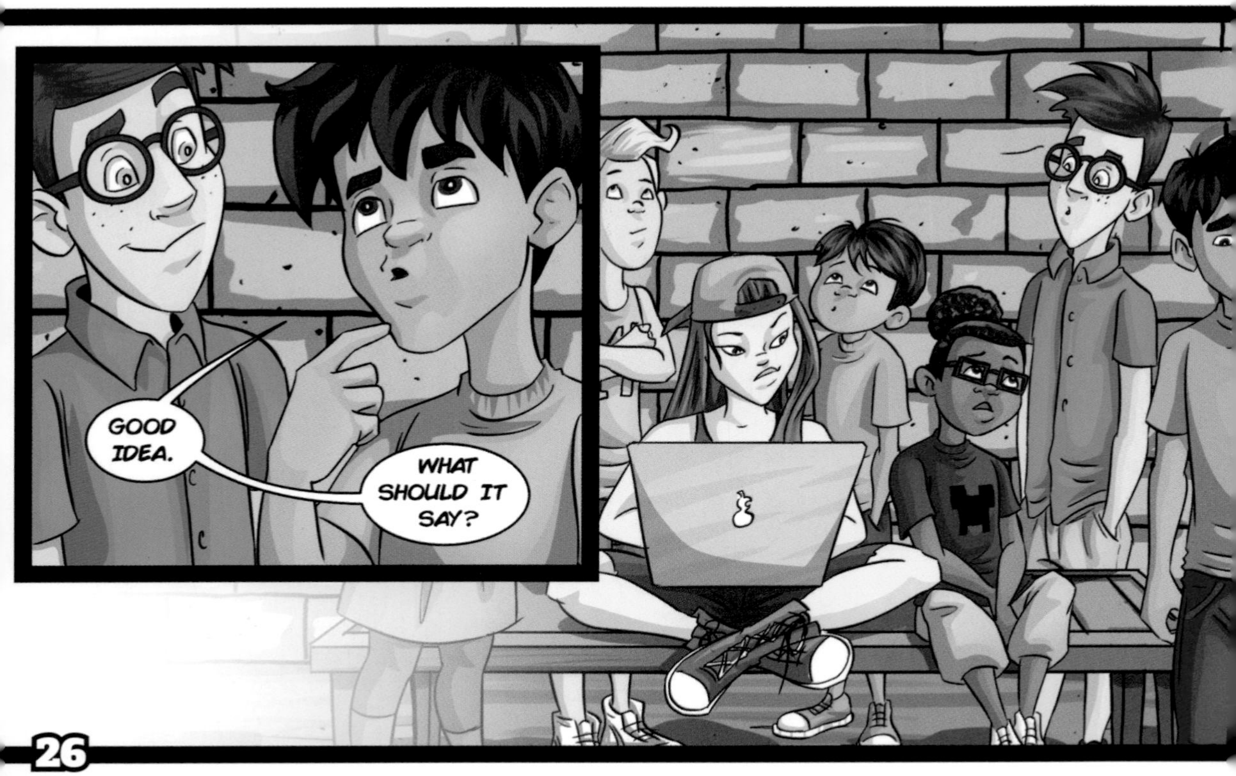
GOOD IDEA.
WHAT SHOULD IT SAY?

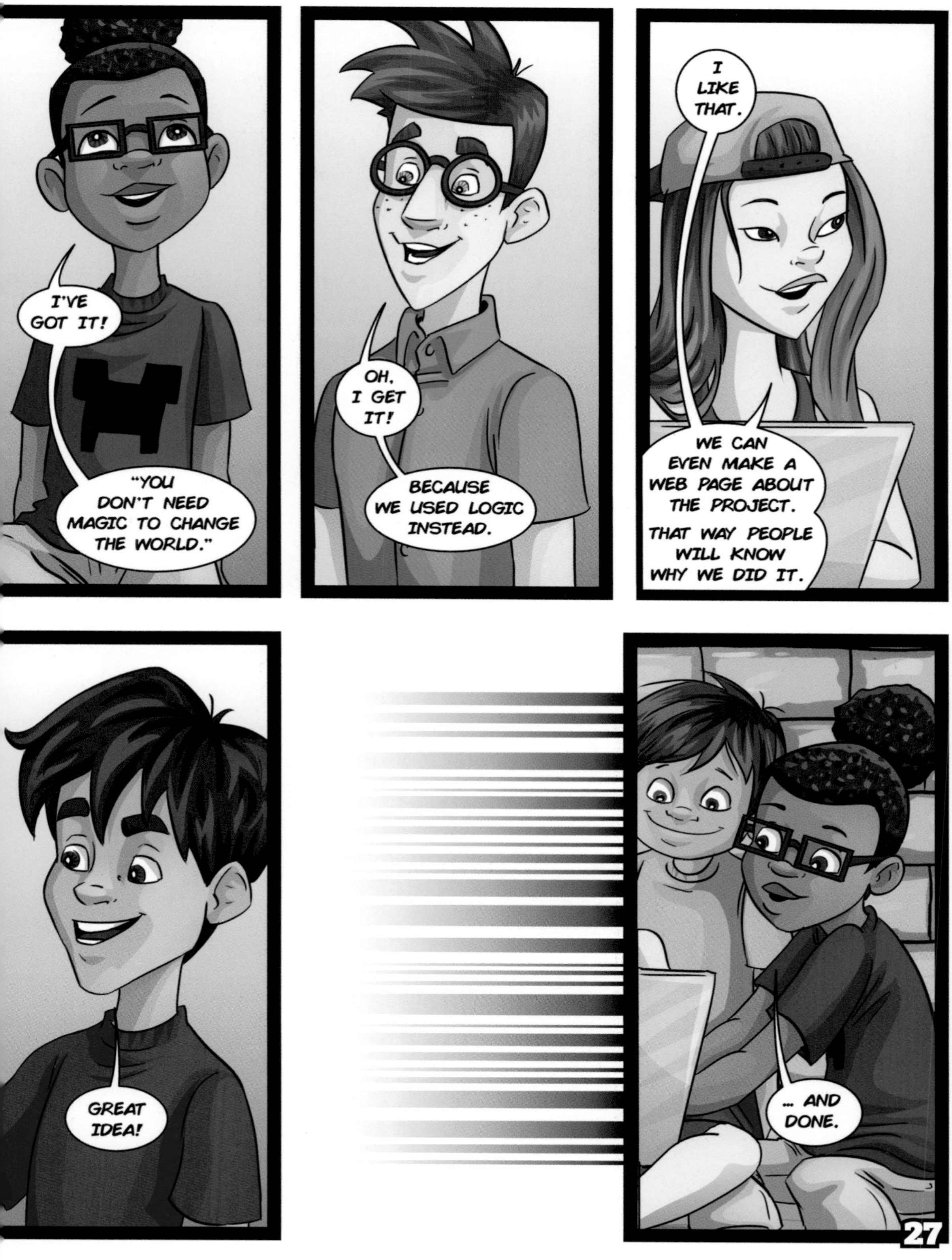
I'VE GOT IT!
"YOU DON'T NEED MAGIC TO CHANGE THE WORLD."
OH, I GET IT!
BECAUSE WE USED LOGIC INSTEAD.
I LIKE THAT.
WE CAN EVEN MAKE A WEB PAGE ABOUT THE PROJECT.
THAT WAY PEOPLE WILL KNOW WHY WE DID IT.
GREAT IDEA!
... AND DONE.

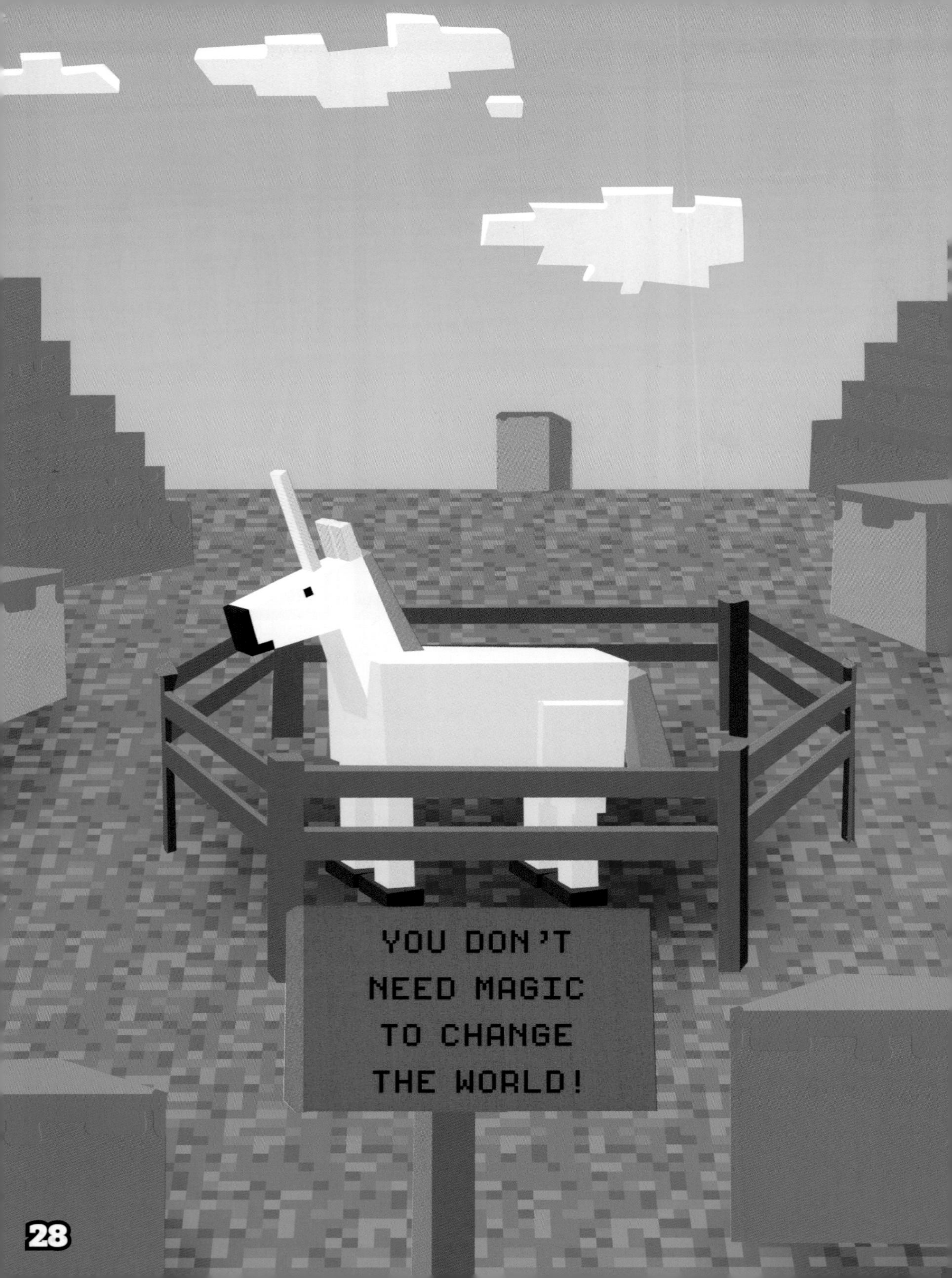
YOU DON'T
NEED MAGIC
TO CHANGE
THE WORLD!

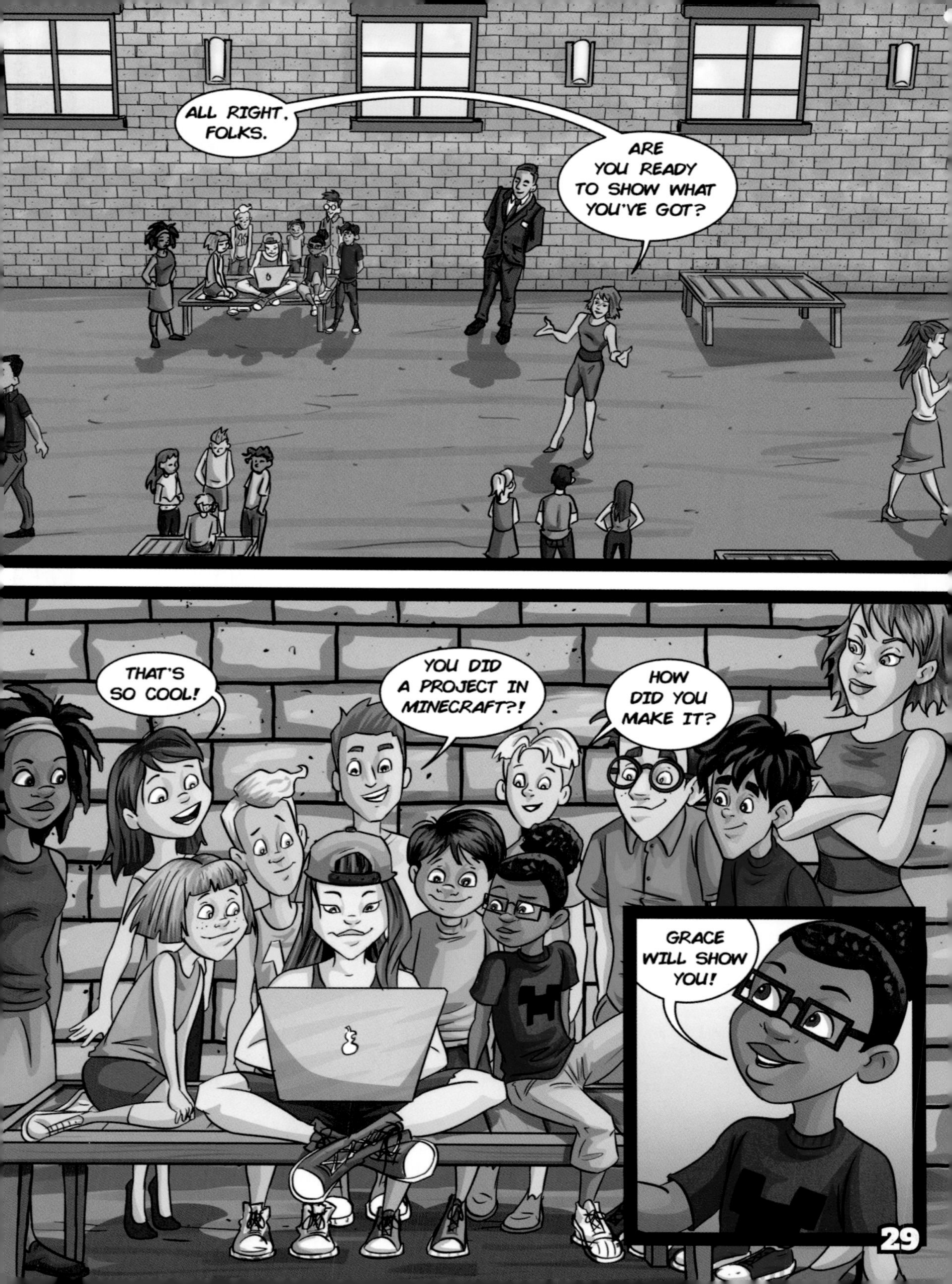
ALL RIGHT, FOLKS.
ARE YOU READY TO SHOW WHAT YOU'VE GOT?
THAT'S SO COOL!
YOU DID A PROJECT IN MINECRAFT?!
HOW DID YOU MAKE IT?
GRACE WILL SHOW YOU!

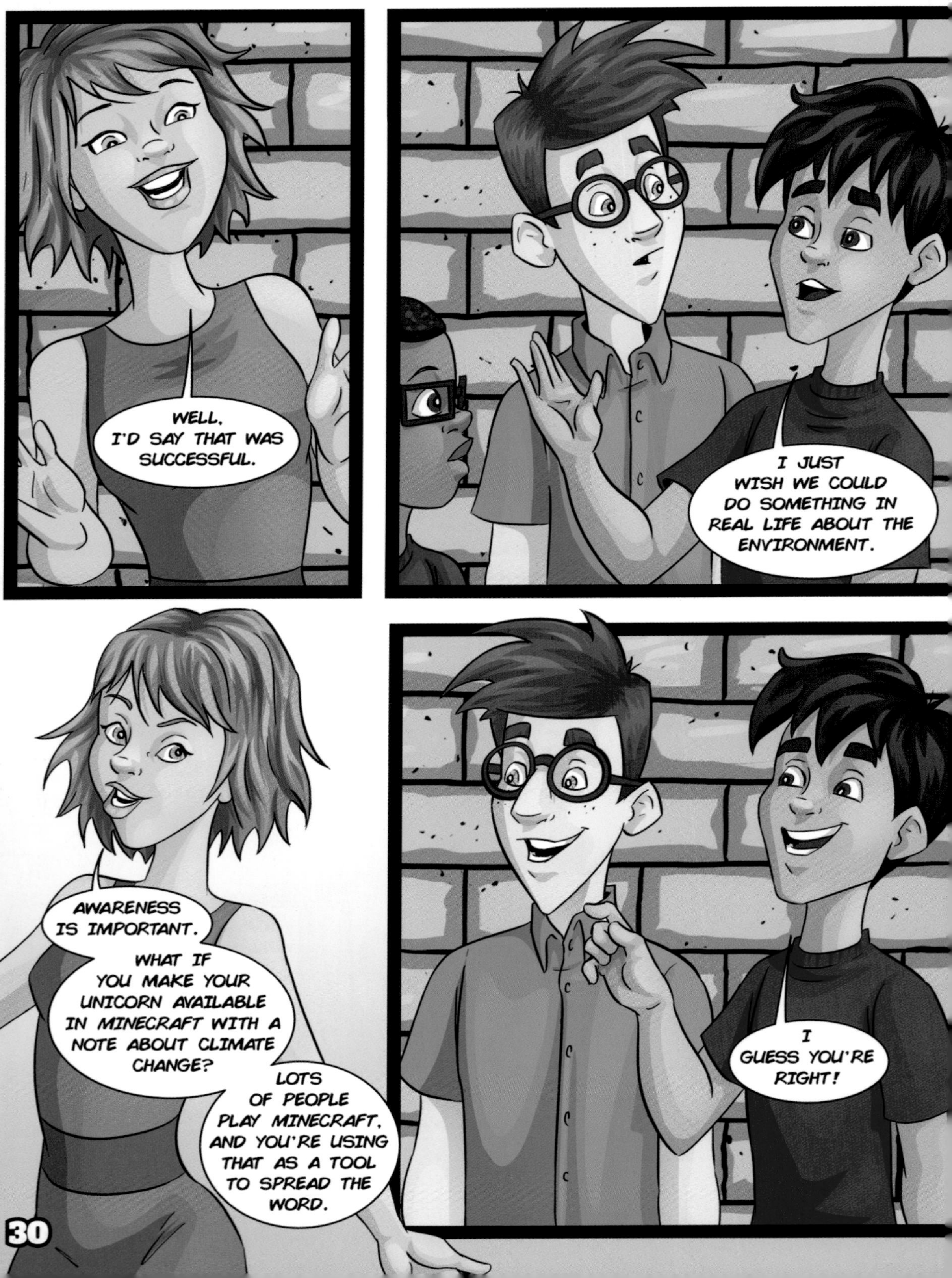
WELL, I'D SAY THAT WAS SUCCESSFUL.
I JUST WISH WE COULD DO SOMETHING IN REAL LIFE ABOUT THE ENVIRONMENT.
AWARENESS IS IMPORTANT.
WHAT IF YOU MAKE YOUR UNICORN AVAILABLE IN MINECRAFT WITH A NOTE ABOUT CLIMATE CHANGE?
LOTS OF PEOPLE PLAY MINECRAFT, AND YOU'RE USING THAT AS A TOOL TO SPREAD THE WORD.
I GUESS YOU'RE RIGHT!

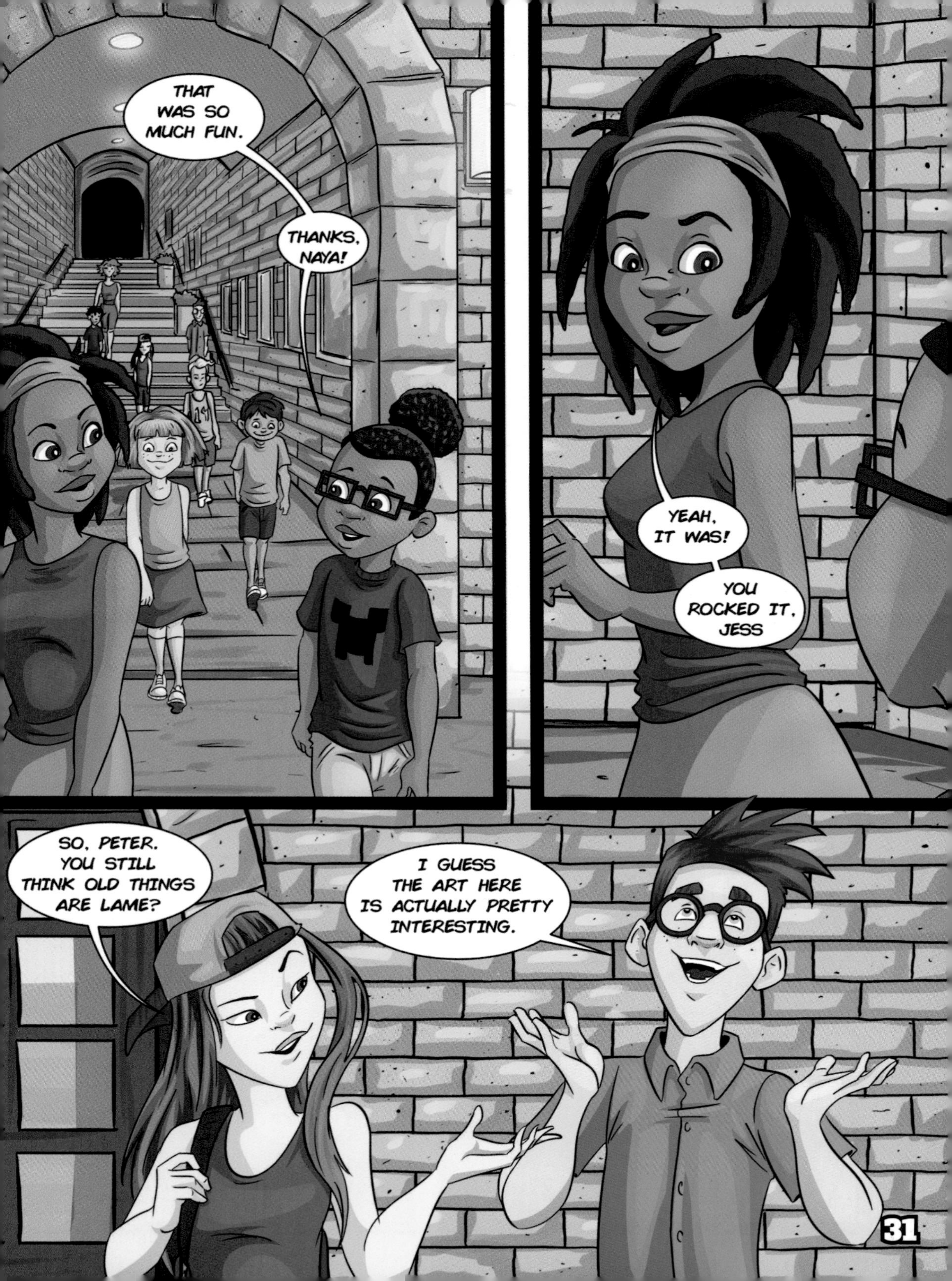

THAT WAS SO MUCH FUN.
THANKS, NAYA!
YEAH, IT WAS!
YOU ROCKED IT, JESS
SO, PETER. YOU STILL THINK OLD THINGS ARE LAME?
I GUESS THE ART HERE IS ACTUALLY PRETTY INTERESTING.

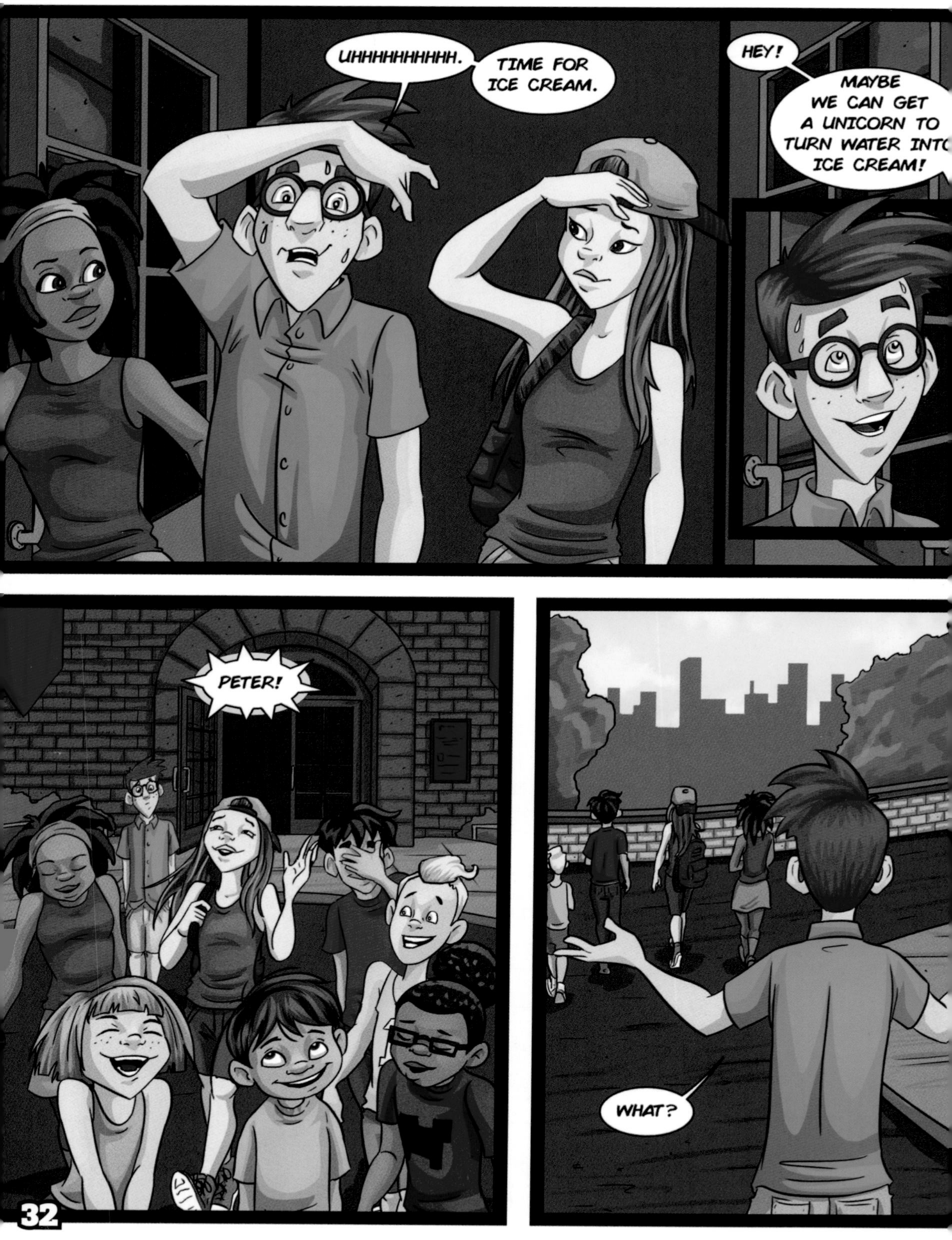
UHHHHHHHHHH.
TIME FOR ICE CREAM.
HEY!
MAYBE WE CAN GET A UNICORN TO TURN WATER INTO ICE CREAM!
PETER!
WHAT?